This novel is entirely a work of fiction. The characters, places and incidents portrayed in it are the work of the author's imagination. Any resemblance to actual persons, living or dead, events or locations is purely coincidental

ISBN: 978-0-6483522-5-9

To Mary
Who helped me find my way in the darkest of times

CHAPTER 1

B lake breathed in a deep breath as he alighted from the taxi. The tang of sea air buzzed in his nostrils and salted his lungs. There was nothing to compare with the piquancy of fresh Aussie ocean breezes to make you glad you were alive.

Blake sighed; the magic wasn't working. Today he would be happy to be alive anywhere, but here, to face his day of reckoning.

His fingers brushed the phone in his pocket. There was hope of redemption. His device held the evidence—evidence that plunged a knife into his heart every time it snuck into his thoughts. He sighed again. He accepted the time had come for the truth to be told—regardless of the consequences. It had taken several months to come to the conclusion he owed his jilted bride no loyalty.

The driver pulled his bags from the boot and stood them at the bottom of the wide sweep of steps leading to the front door.

Blake paid him, with a tip.

The driver laughed. "Been in the States, mate?"

"Hawaii for a few of months. Developed the habit. Never mind keep it, anyway. Buy yourself a beer."

"Thanks." The driver hopped back into the car and drove away.

Blake picked up his bags and climbed the white stairs with slow heavy steps. He kept glancing up to the imposing front doors fully expecting hell to descend on his head once they realized he had arrived.

He had ascended almost halfway when the door flung open. In anticipation he paused. His youngest stepsister hurtled with lithe grace down the steps balancing precariously in her six-inch heels. He flinched inwardly, unsure of his reception.

"You're here. You're finally home, big brother," Rhiana screamed.

Relief wafted over him melting some of the stinging needles of tension. At least one of his stepsisters could bear to welcome him. He doubted Talisha would be so forgiving about the tangle of lies and public humiliation he had left behind when he bolted.

He dropped his bags and held his arms wide. "Crikey, Rhiana, I swear you've grown more stunning in the past few months, if that is at all possible."

She giggled as she launched herself into his embrace. "You don't look too bad yourself, big brother, even with the designer face hair and man bun."

Blake squeezed her tightly against his chest. "How's Dad?"

She pulled away and shook her head. "Oh God, Blake, we thought he would die." The sparkle in her green eyes faded and tears sprang unbidden. "He's just a shadow of himself. The heart attack and the surgery took the life out of him."

Worry about his father's severe heart attack and ongoing problems clenched Blake in a tangle of fear, regrets and guilt. "I should have come sooner. If he had…"

"He didn't and you're here now, that's all that matters."

Blake grimaced. Guilt still seared his gut with sharp pinpricks.

"Come on inside. Mum's got some lunch ready then we can go into the hospital to see Dad. They moved him from ICU this morning. Regardless of your indiscretion, he's missed you so much."

"Yes, I know. I've missed you all too." Blake bent down and hefted his case.

Rhiana bounced up the steps beside him. "You know you have to provide answers, big brother. The debacle you caused is not forgotten or forgiven."

"I know, but not right now." Obviously, he carried all the blame. His jilted bride had not owned up.

Rhiana scuttled up the steps, the sharp staccato of her heels snapping in the still air. She made no attempt to help him with his luggage.

Not that he had much. He wasn't sure how long he was staying.

His stepmother appeared at the door and the delicious aroma of freshly baked scones wafted on the hot air. Alice had aged. Gray faded her beautiful auburn hair at the temples and the lines around her mouth and eyes had become more pronounced. His father's illness had taken a hefty toll on her.

Guilt stabbed through him. He smiled. "Hi Alice, been baking?"

"Of course, Blake, isn't that what mothers do?"

He pushed away the faint protest that hovered on his lips because it was petty and childish. *Why can't I just accept Alice's mothering.* "When the prodigal son returns bringing his shame with him? You sure you have it right?"

"Yes, Blake, I have it perfectly correct."

"I'm not going to be pilloried for daring to show my face?"

His stepmother smiled. "Not by me, Blake."

He grimaced. "Maybe not, but I'm sure there are plenty of others, ahead of you in the queue, baying for my blood."

A touch of wistfulness shadowed her expression.

Guilt squeezed again. He hadn't meant to sound sarcastic. He regretted refusing to accept her as a mother for she had shown herself to be a good woman and devoted to his father. *She has seen my father through the shambles I left behind and through his illness and brush with death.* He hated himself for hurting her once again.

"Alice..."

She shook her head. "Come on in, Blake, lunch is ready, and your father is waiting to see you."

Blake dropped his suitcases in the wide sunlight foyer and followed the two women through the house. Nothing had changed but it felt different—an emptiness lurked in the luxurious abode.

Guilt dug deep inside. He should have come home earlier instead of sulking in hiding, but even now he wished he hadn't. Being away had given him a modicum of distance from the pain and humiliation of seeing his bride clothed in her wedding gown fucking Connor, his best man, and his closest mate since kindergarten, barely an hour before the ceremony.

With not a word to anyone he'd been on his way to the airport by the time the organ started to play in the church. He still ached from Stephanie's ruthless betrayal and ultimate rejection. Yet despite the hurt he couldn't say with any conviction that he didn't still love her. He cursed his weakness, especially now he'd come back to Adelaide to face the inevitable explanations that would be required.

He stepped into the familiar kitchen, but it didn't feel like home. Alice served up fresh rolls and the fillings on a platter. Blake helped himself to a roll and filled it with generous helpings of ham and salad. As they ate Alice filled him in on the details of his father's heart attack and what they had done to fix the problem. Blake was shocked at his father's decline but he shouldn't have been. His father had always been a workaholic and never made any attempt to take care of his health. He had once smoked heavily and didn't really eat a healthy diet. He loved his wine and whiskey and therefore carried a bit of extra weight.

Blake had often told him to slow down and smell the roses but his father had laughed his urging off stating he thrived on the manic pace of controlling his construction business and property portfolio. He had been disappointed when Blake had chosen to take up law and begin his own practice with his close friend Callum instead of stepping into the family business.

"Well, if you've finished, we should get going to the hospital."

Blake smiled at his stepmother. "Nice lunch Alice, thanks. I've had plenty. I'll unpack when I get back."

"I've put you in the front guest room Blake. I thought you might prefer it."

Relief washed over Blake. "Thanks Alice. I definitely would be more comfortable there."

With the dishes loaded in the dishwasher they piled into the car and headed into town.

Blake had never been to the new Royal Adelaide Hospital, so he followed Alice's lead up six floors and down the long corridors.

His father lay in the hospital bed with his eyes closed. Machines beeped and puffed. He looked a frail, haggard caricature of the once towering, robust and imposing man he had always been.

The reality of his father's condition hit home. Blake gasped, hesitated then stepped forward to embrace him.

His eyes few open. "Blake, at long last. I'm so glad you have finally come home." His father grunted. "I'm still a bit sore."

Blake released his hold. "Sorry Dad, I didn't think. How are you? Really?"

"I'm as weak as a kitten. Thought my number had come up. God damn it, never had such pain."

"I should have been here..."

His father smiled. "You're here now, Blake, that's what matters."

Embarrassment and pain washed over him as his father's voice faded, cracked, and then went silent. After what seemed like an eternity, his father cleared his throat. "You know we'll have to talk, son, about the mess you left behind."

"I know Dad and I'm sorry," Blake said.

"It's all right son, but an explanation would be nice."

No, it's bloody not. They're walking on eggshells. Just waiting for me to... to what? Say something brilliant that would fix the past? Well, he couldn't.

"We'll discuss that later, but I do have something to talk to you about."

Blake knew what was coming. He was prepared for it. "I know Dad, you want me to take over the business; well at least until you are back on your feet."

His father reached out and laid his hand on Blake's arm. "Son, I'm never going to be able to go back to what I was doing. It is time for me to retire and smell those damn roses you've been telling me about for years. If I had listened to you and Alice before I might not be in this predicament."

"Dad."

"Look son, I know you have your practice and that law is your first love but if I can have some time to make suitable arrangements. William and Linley need some guidance, but they might eventually take over. I don't know. But we have three big jobs that need finishing. One has issues. I know it's a big ask son, but will you consider giving your old man a break?"

Blake took a deep breath and rested his hand on his father's. "Dad don't worry yourself. I'll take on the business. I've already talked to Callum. I decided after the Rochester case I don't want to spend my life defending criminals and low life's, especially when we make a mistake like Billy Rochester. I've already sold my half of the firm to Callum and he's bringing in his twin siblings Ruth and David, both just graduated from law school, as associates."

"Blake!"

Blake turned at Rhiana's exclamation.

"But you always loved the law, Blake. It was your practice; your baby."

Blake shrugged, grimaced and turned back to his father.

His father looked agitated. "Are you sure Blake? I don't want you making irreversible decisions like that just for me."

Blake was concerned about the effect his news would have on his father's condition. He hastened to reassure him. "Dad this decision was made before you got ill. I've made the right decision."

A doctor appeared at the door. "I think Mr. Gifford as had enough for one day. We don't want to set his recovery back. We are hoping he can go home on Saturday under My Home Hospital care, but he needs to rest and not, Mr. Gifford, worrying about everything, including your business."

His father nodded. He looked up at Blake. "Can you meet with William, Linley and my solicitor, Lyall tomorrow and get a handle on what needs to be done. There is a stack of files on my desk, they will give you the background information you'll need."

Blake stood up and squeezed his father's hand. "You rest Dad, don't worry. I'll sort it all out."

His father nodded and closed his eyes. "Thank you, son." His words were barely a whisper.

Blake's spirit was crushed and broken. His father had always been his tower of strength, robust, strong, and determined. Seeing his father like this was heartbreaking.

Alice paused for a moment once she was seated in the car. "Thank you, Blake for taking on the business. He's been fretting about it so much I'm sure it's interfered with his recovery."

Blake nodded. "It probably has. Well now he can rest."

Alice started the car then looked across at Blake. "Are you sure you want to give up law and take up the business?"

Blake nodded. "I can't let Dad down and I'm at a loose end right now." He smiled at Alice.

She nodded and smiled back.

The drive back to the house was done in relative silence. Everyone's thoughts whirling back to the hospital and Muir.

The next few days were a fast rotation of visiting his father and getting his head around the business. It was a steep learning curve, but William and Linley were thorough with his induction. By Friday his head was spinning with details of the business in general and specifically the three big jobs. To clear his head, he began running along the beach every morning just as it was getting light. He felt very out of his depth in the construction industry.

The atmosphere in the house changed when his father arrived home on Saturday morning with Alice concentrating her efforts on her husband. Blake spent most of Saturday going through files and contracts compiling a list of questions for William and Linley on Monday along with other issues he wanted to delve into more thoroughly.

Sunday, he rose in the predawn darkness, dressed in shorts and tank top and walked out onto the empty beach. The waves splashed lightly onto the sand but otherwise everything was quiet and still. He headed for the distance Henley Beach jetty breathing evenly and running lightly in the damp sand at the water's edge. He tried to shut his mind off from the business and concentrate on the moment. So far nothing further had been said about his disastrous wedding ending, but he knew it would have to be faced eventually. At the jetty he turned and jogged back to his father's house.

He snuck inside but stopped in surprise to find Brianna already dressed and in the kitchen. She looked sulky sitting at the table with a glass of juice. Blake filled a glass for himself and slid into a chair opposite her.

"What's up Sis?"

Rhiana pouted. "Mum promised to take me to the market this morning, but she can't leave Dad, so I can't go."

"Can't you drive yourself?"

Rhiana frowned. "I haven't got my license yet. I have more practice hours to do because when Dad got sick my lessons stopped."

"So, what's so important about the market then?"

"I always buy organic stuff for me, better and cheaper than the supermarket and they will be good for Dad. I also put my name down for a cooking class."

Blake looked his sister over feeling sorry for her. Her stepfather's illness had also affected her significantly. "Well, I suppose I could take you."

Rhiana instantly perked up. "Would you?"

Blake downed his juice. "Give me time to shower and I'll take you."

Rhiana jumped up and hugged him. "Thank you, Blake."

Rhiana pointed out 'her' car in the garage. His father had obviously done for her as he had for him and Talisha and invested in a mid-range car for them to learn in and drive while they were at uni.

"You're driving cos I'm not making a habit for being your chauffer."

Rhiana pouted.

"Don't look at me like that little sis. I'll be a kind tutor. You need to do this; so up you hop into the driver's seat."

Blake grinned to himself as she took the keys and obediently climbed into the car.

CHAPTER 2

Tya pressed the send button and sat back. She stretched her arms above her head watching as the stream of email invitations to the Sydney Trade Show scattered into cyber space. With that task finished she closed her laptop and spun her comfortable leather chair away from her desk.

She still had time to go to the Thistle Street garden before night fell. She loved these long summer evenings made possible by daylight saving time changes. It had been almost thirty-eight degrees today, but it was cooler now with a slight sea breeze.

She pushed out of the chair, grabbed her shoes and bag slipped out of the front door. The door squeaked and stuck when she went to close it, but with a solid tug she pulled it shut. The timber frames of the windows next to the door rattled in response. Tya sighed, the house needed so much work, but it all cost money she didn't have.

With her virtual PA business growing slowly and her jewelry sales she had enough to pay the bills and accumulate small amounts of savings to plough back into her home. Good honest money from good honest labor. She shuddered. Not like her mother.

She paused on the footpath and took an appraising look at her home. By budgeting carefully she'd managed to fix the roof and the plumbing since she inherited it. It didn't matter that it was shabby.

Satisfied with her assessment she walked briskly down her street and around the corner. Two streets on the right lay Thistle Street. She'd discovered the unused block behind the fence twelve months ago smothered in kikuyu so wild it reached four foot up the back fence. She'd watched the block for a couple of months. Finally satisfied the owners had abandoned it she slipped behind the fence with a couple of her friends and cleared the weeds. Nobody interfered with their work. No one told them to leave, and no-one claimed ownership.

They cleared the land then re-cycled some old railway sleepers and built garden beds. Eventually they filled the beds with soil they scrounged from a friendly builder digging out a large site. He also gave them the pallets to build a compost system and everyone around contributed to the input of organic material. It had taken nearly twelve months but at last they had a thriving garden.

The six foot stone fence cutting the garden off from the street loomed up, imposing in the shadowy light of dusk. Tya slipped through the wrought iron gate that squeaked on opening. The splash of running water danced between the plants. Tya followed the sound through the rows and rows of tomatoe plants towering over her head and weighed down by fruit of varying colors from green to almost red.

The ghostly shape of Endeva threaded her way between the cucumber trellis' tenderly winding the new tendrils around the mesh to encourage the plants to climb.

"Hi Endeva, how goes it tonight?"

The gray headed woman nodded. "Well, Tya, we'll have a bumper crop for the market on Sunday."

"Even after we fill ten boxes for the woman's shelter and those with their names on the list?"

Endeva smiled. "Of course, and plenty of strawberries too for those poor little kiddies. They love a feed of strawberries."

Tya turned on the second tap and picked up the hose. As she watched the crystal clear stream gush out of the hose and turn the rich dark earth into mud, she wondered why the owner of this deserted block behind the wall hadn't noticed the high water usage and come to investigate.

With the whole three-quarter acre block covered in food bearing crops they had enough to supply the local women's shelter and some of the poorer families struggling to make ends meet in the surrounding area. They often had enough to sell at the market to bring in cash to replenish essentials such as compost, mulch and seedlings. It was never much, and they had always managed but their major problem at the moment was the antiquated rotary hoe. It had died and could not be revived. Tya didn't know how they would replace it.

In the last two years Tya and her friends had taken over two other blocks and encouraged the community, mostly single mums, and unemployed, to come and help cultivate the land. It not only gave them a sense of industry but pride as they carried home boxes of vegetables and fruit they helped to grow.

She started when Endeva touched her shoulder.

"Time to finish up, too dark to see now, love," Endeva said.

"I know, I will come early tomorrow and get some more done."

Endeva wound the hose up. "Good, then you can supervise Luke and that young whipper snapper, Jordan, while they spread the compost in the back bed and get the next crop of corn and tomatoes planted. They tend to muck around if nobody's about."

"They're young, Endeva, and haven't ever had a scrap of discipline in their short lives so we should be grateful they are motivated to be here at all."

The older woman patted her arm. "I know, love, they're good lads on the whole."

Tya shut the gate behind them then tucked her arm in Endeva's as they walked down the dark street. "We've been lucky despite the unlocked gate to have only been robbed of produce once and more surprisingly never vandalized. I must have more faith in humankind." *Not likely in this lifetime. I've seen too much already.* She often cursed her own cynicism, but having lived in the street of hard knocks beginning right in the hospital ward the day she was born it had become instinctive.

"We're very lucky, but most of the locals appreciate us." Endeva kissed her cheeks. "Sleep well, Tya.

Tya stood by her gate and watched as Endeva walked three houses down and into her own place before she walked up her garden path already pulling the key out of her pocket.

"So, where you been? Never here when your poor old mum needs ya."

Tya started back teetering on the edge of the top step of the verandah.

The owner of the voice moved from the deep shadows at the end of the verandah. Her mother.

Clothed in a bright pink tubular dress, barely long enough to cover her backside, her ample bust spilled over the strapless neckline. Her long tresses dyed platinum blonde.

Unease and angst washed over Tya in equal measure. "What do you want?"

"What ya think I want? Business is slow. I need money. You owe me, Tya, you with your quaint little house and stalls at the market. You can afford to help ya Mum."

"I don't owe you anything, Mum."

The shadowy figure stepped forward. "You'd sing a different tune, my girl, if you had to go on the game to feed yourself."

"Mum, I can give you food. I wouldn't see you starve, but I will not give you money."

Her mother lurched forward her hand raised to slap Tya. Tya jumped back.

Her mother pushed past her, stumbled down the path and out the gate. She paused on the footpath. "You'll regret this, my girl. I'll see you do."

In the harsh glare of the street light Tya saw her mother's distended stomach. The pink material strained over it. It could be mistaken for a fat tummy, but Tya knew it wasn't. Her mother's scrawny frame didn't have an ounce of fat on it. Tya wondered how she hid the signs of her drug use from the johns well enough for her to do any business at all and having a baby bump probably didn't help. Christ didn't she know how to protect herself. Four kids already. Damn it, four ruined lives and now another poor little mite destined to inherit self-destructive genes and the miserable horror called 'life'.

Tya stomach wrenched and heaved as she slipped inside her sanctuary and slammed the door on the outside world. No matter how determinedly she tried to leave her wretched past behind, it continued to haunt and hurt her. She didn't know how to vanquish it or how to accept it. Filled with frustration and angst, she threw herself on the bed stinging tears burning trails down her cheeks and wracking sobs cramping her chest.

***

The market already bustled with stall holders setting up, vans and trailers being backed into place and gazebos and tables erected.

Dave arrived with coffee as Tya put the finishing touches on the display. She sank down into her folding chair and sipped her coffee. Although the gates had just opened quite a few customers strolled around inspecting the produce available and as usual they did an early roaring trade—they had a reputation for the best veggies at the market. As Tya expected they almost immediately sold all the punnets of strawberries on the table.

"I'll get some more, Endeva, if you can hold the fort. We need them before Dave gets back."

"Can you manage?"

"No problems. They're not heavy, just awkward to carry. I won't be long."

Tya hurried up the gravel path towards Dave's van. She wished they could park closer, but with the increased interest by stall holders meant they could no longer get their vehicle in by the stall once they had unloaded and set up.

She swung open the door and selected the top tray. She stepped back from the van juggling the tray and the keys.

"Uffff." The heavy door of the van thudded into her shoulder.

Two mountain bikes whizzed past her.

Tya struggled to keep her footing. She grabbed for the side of the van as her feet slipped in the dirt and her legs crumpled at the knees. The tray flew from her hands, rocketed through the air, and landed upside down in the dirt. Punnets of strawberries scattered, some flying open scattering lush berries on to the dirt. Her ankle wrenched sideways. She tumbled forward gasping in pain as the hard dirt rose up to meet her. As she reached out to save herself from swaying sideways, she unexpectedly slammed into a solid but movable object.

It swayed with the force of her connection then steadied. Strong muscular arms embraced her as she scuttled her feet to regain her balance.

"Hang on, we're going down."

The husky male voice rumbled in her ear. His scent tantalized her. The warmth of his body seeped into hers through the thinness of her dress. She latched onto hard muscular arms as they tumbled toward the ground.

He hit the ground hard and the air in his lungs expelled under force. He still held her in a firm embrace but grunted as her weight thudded against his chest.

They lay in a tangle of arms, legs and broken agapanthus plants.

Tya gasped for breath. "I'm so sorry." She tried to extract herself but only succeeded in pressing closer to him and heightening her awareness of his masculine form. She looked directly at him.

He made no attempt to release her. His mouth curled up in a rueful smile, squaring his strong jaw and showing white teeth. His dark honey blond hair swept back from his forehead in a bun and his neatly trimmed designer stubble highlighted the even olive tones of his skin and the angular shape of his jaw.

"Are you all right?"

"I turned my ankle as I fell, but otherwise I'm okay thanks to you. What about you?"

"A bruise or two and dented pride, but otherwise I'm fine. Here let me help you up."

He gripped her arms and assisted her to slide off his body. Freed of her weight he stood in one lithe movement then reached down to her. With a firm grip he helped her rise.

Tya tried to put her foot to the ground. "Owww." She would have unbalanced except for his strong hold on her arm.

"You're hurt. Can you walk? If not, I'll carry you."

"You don't have to do that. I don't have far to go." Tya pointed to the stall.

"No arguments, it could be broken. You took quite a tumble." He reached down and scooped her up into his arms.

She looked up into his face.

He grinned, his grey eyes sparkling. "Blake Gifford, at your service. It's not often I get to save a beautiful woman in distress."

A tingle of awareness scattered through her at his blatant flirting. She couldn't find anything sensible to respond with. Her heart beat in an uneven rhythm behind her left breast as it pressed against his chest. The warmth of his body seeped through the thinness of her dress bringing hyper awareness of his maleness.

His steady, solid hold as he strode with athletic ease across the uneven ground made her feel lightheaded but safe.

Dave waved them over.

Blake turned in the direction of the stall.

Endeva pushed forward the sturdiest chair.

Blake tenderly placed her in it.

Tya looked up at him. "Thank you for saving me, Mr. Gifford."

"Make it, Blake, and I didn't really save you, or the strawberries." He knelt on the ground and gently eased her shoe off.

Tya winced.

"Sorry." He tenderly examined her ankle.

His fingertips slid across her skin leaving a blazing trail of awareness.

"I don't think it's broken. Just sprained." He looked around at Dave. "Do you have some ice?"

Dave handed over the bundle of ice he had already prepared.

As Blake arranged the package around her ankle Tya sat mesmerized by the man kneeling in front of her. The width of his shoulders, the muscular arms and shapely muscles stretching his shirt made a sculptured body with perfect proportions that gave off an aura of confidence and untamed masculinity with a touch of gentleness from his long shapely fingers touching her skin. Primeval warmth flowed through her. This sort of man she could be interested in but couldn't contemplate—not with her background.

In an attempt to douse her sexual musings, she tore her gaze away from him and looked back at the strawberries scattered on the ground. "Damn kids on bikes. They aren't supposed to ride them here on market days. Look at all my strawberries."

He touched her arm lightly. "I'll help pick them up. Most of them could be used for jam."

"Who wants to make jam?" Dave asked.

Blake glanced at the spilled berries. "My stepmother will make fresh homemade organic jam for my sister. I'll pay premium price for them, just tell me how much."

The warm gravelly timbre of his voice grazed across her tingling emotions heightening her awareness of his closeness. She swallowed and licked her dry lips. "I can't charge you full price. It wasn't your fault, and you did save me from a nasty landing. You can have them."

He grinned, shook his head, then reached into the pocket on the side of his shorts and pulled out a leather wallet. He extracted a fifty dollar note. "Here this should cover the damage. I'll go help your friend retrieve the fruit."

Her skin buzzed as their hands connected around the money. He stared down at her, his grey eyes flickering with light and shadow. She held her breath in anticipation. He moved closer. Of its own volition her body leaned toward him. The air between them sizzled with awareness. Her heart pattered in an uneven rhythm.

"Oh, there you are, Blake, I thought I'd lost you in the crowd."

He started back letting her hand slip from his. "Give us a minute, Sis."

He turned and walked towards Dave.

Tya's breath caught in her throat. Her heart did a little dance in her chest, sending tingling vibes running along her nerve endings to pool between her legs as she had her first good look at him. Definitely not the average male at well over six feet and the carefully sculptured body—chiseled and curved into a replica of a Greek God. Soft grey eyes one could swim in and a smile that would warm the coldest heart. That perfect body encased in stylishly tailored khaki shorts and a clinging rust colored singlet top that clung to his curves and angles. Even the green swipes of agapanthus juice couldn't take away from his sexiness. In fact, they emphasized his shapely butt and broad shoulders. He moved with a leisurely stride that tightened the shorts against his thighs and backside with each step and each curve of the muscles across his back accentuated by the soft material molding against his flesh.

He bent down to collect the spilled fruit.

Tya watched him appreciating every move he made.

They brought the salvage for her to inspect. Some of the fruit had extensive damage and was beyond help, but others had remained encased in their clear clamshell packaging.

She picked over the loose berries. "Are you sure you want the damaged ones?"

"All they need is a wash and most of them will be good as new," Dave said.

"Dave's right most of them just need a wash. It won't matter in jam if they are a bit bruised." Blake smiled.

Tya's heart lurched. She had never reacted this way to a man before. She shook her head to clear it. "Fine, if you're happy about the deal. Dave, can you re-pack them, please."

"Blake."

Blake placed the tray on the trestle and turned to Rhiana. "I'm all yours now, Sis."

Tya looked in the direction of the strident, little girl voice she recognized. Rhiana Tennyson-Gifford, one of her regular customers, tottered toward her on six-inch stilettos. Her calf length lemon yellow skirt clung tightly to her curves and the white crop top barely came below her voluptuous bust showing a bare midriff. Tya caught the sparkle of the diamond in her navel. *So he's her brother, interesting.*

"Do hurry up, Blake or all the good stuff will be gone," The young woman beckoned. "Hi ladies. Do you still have something left for me?"

"I...we..." Tya's voice cracked and faded as her gaze locked with his.

"Of course, we do. What are you looking for today? The usual?" Endeva stepped forward smiling at the sexy young female teetering in front of their stall.

"I didn't think I would make it today. But my big brother finally gave into my whining and brought me. Anyway, I'll have some kale, cucumbers and of course strawberries..."

Tya vaguely heard the woman rattling on through the haze of awareness that held her paralyzed.

He stepped up beside the woman until his thighs rested against the edge of the table, the movement emphasized his crotch.

Tya struggled but finally managed to lift her gaze to meet his direct look.

He laughed at her, an almost imperceptible chuckle.

Heat raced through her and her face flushed hot. Blast, he knew—he did it deliberately.

With a delicate grip he picked up a tomato in each hand. His long shapely fingers embraced the rich red fruit. He very gently stroked the skin with his thumb as he pretended to weigh them up against each other.

"Mmmm – firm, plump, and a perfect handful." He caressed the tomatoes but stared at her.

Desire scorched through her. She swallowed, licked her lips with the tip of her tongue and lowered her eyes only to find herself staring directly at his crotch again. Shudders tore through her as she ripped her gaze away and brought it back to his face. She gripped the edge of the table as sexual heat coursed through her body. His scent wafted around her—sharp, spicy, and all male. Of freshly washed skin, the overlying tang of cologne and a faint whiff of agapanthus.

Oh my God – I'm gonna orgasm right here – and he hasn't even touched me.

He never took his gaze off her as he replaced the tomatoes on the table. He picked up a zucchini and turned it round and round.

Tya gasped in a tight breath of air, choked on it, coughed and let the shudders of arousal rumbled through her.

He put the zucchini down as he raised his eyebrows just a little then slid both hands deep into his pockets.

Tya licked her lips again.

As he turned away Endeva leaned in close. "Hey, put your tongue back in, missy, it ain't yours."

Tya flapped her hand at Endeva and continued to perve and drool.

"Blake, please hold these bags for me while I get some money."

Without hesitation Blake dragged his hands out of his pockets and took the two bags in one hand and the box of damaged strawberries Dave had packed for him in the other. He seemed untouched by their latest encounter, but the slight smile and simmering look in his eyes indicated he knew all too well the experience had left Tya shattered and aroused.

"I'll put these in the cooler and meet you for a coffee after you finish your class."

"Okay. Rhiana handed over her money and with a little wave she tottered off in the direction of the pavilion.

Tya sagged back in the chair.

"Do you want to explain?"

Tya looked up at Endeva. "Sure. Two young idiots on mountains bikes crashed into me. I dropped the strawberries and fell into *his* arms as he came around the corner of the van and we both ended up sprawled in the agapanthus bed."

"Yeah, I saw you, on top of him. Looked right cozy, it did," Dave said.

"Dave, it wasn't like that at all, although I wouldn't mind getting that close again in the right circumstances. He's gorgeous, feels good, smells good and seems very caring. He even took the strawberries at full price for his stepmother to make organic jam for his cute little sister."

"Wishful thinking, missy. He isn't for the likes of you."

"I know, Endeva, but a woman is still entitled to dream a little."

"As long as it's only dreaming."

Coldness trickled through her. *Damn my background. Damn my mother.*

CHAPTER 3

After Blake placed Rhiana's purchases in the ice box and while she went to her class he wandered around the market. He bought himself some juice and found a shady spot under the trees not far from the pavilion. He stared into space, his mind wistfully reviewing his time in Hawaii saving the turtles and what he now faced. He wasn't particularly enjoying managing the business and, in the shadows, lurked the inevitable day he would have to face Stephanie.

"Blake, we must go back to the stall. I have just been given the most divine recipe for a corn and zucchini frittata. I got corn but not zucchinis."

Blake started. Rhiana tottered toward him papers clutched in one hand and a plastic take away container in the other. Her handbag dangled precariously from her shoulder.

"Really, Sis?"

"Really, Blake. If you can't be bothered, I'll go by myself."

Blake grinned and shook his head as he jumped out of the chair eager to return to the stall and flirt some more with the gorgeous Tya. *If I play my cards right, I might get a date...maybe more. No, that wouldn't be wise—until I've sorted out my feelings for Stephanie.*

He had no trouble keeping up with his sister over the uneven ground despite her experience with high heels.

Awareness shimmied across his skin. As he approached the stall, he studied her. The white, blonde hair, short and spiked, moist dewy lips.

Long lashes fluttered as she met his direct stare.

The tantalizing swell of her breasts peeping above the modest neckline of her dress held his gaze for a moment before he looked directly at her and grinned. He guessed she stood at only about five foot two. Petite, but sturdy.

She rose with graceful moves from her chair and limped up to the trestle. She looked up and smiled. "Did you forget something?"

Rhiana hurried forward. "Not really. I did the workshop in the pavilion, and I want some zucchini to try the recipe at home. Do you have any left? Two should be enough."

Blake watched Tya lean sideways and scoop up two plump green zucchinis. She handled the fruit gently but with confidence. Long slim fingers flicked open the bag and slid the zucchini in.

She glanced up directly at him. "No after effects?"

He grimaced. "I think I might have a couple of bruises on my back by tomorrow. How's the ankle feeling?"

She smiled. "Not bad with the ice and a couple of painkillers. Endeva will be back in a moment, and I'll sit with it up. Thank you again...Blake. Without you my fall would have been much worse."

He grinned. "Glad to be of service. I'll bring you a jar of jam when it's made."

"I would enjoy that, thanks."

The tinkle of coins hitingt the ground broke the spell holding Tya.

"Holy shit. No," Rhiana spat as she grabbed her brother's arm. "Bugga, she's headed this way."

Blake pulled away. "What the heck has got into you?"

"Stay here, Blake, I'll head her off..."

"Who off?" he asked turning to look.

Talisha and Stephanie were pushing their way toward them through the crowd of shoppers milling around the market.

"Damn, just what I need."

"Hey, Tya," Rhiana pointed at the collection tin on the table. "I'll donate five hundred dollars to your rotary hoe fund if you pretend to be my brother's girlfriend and give him a big smacker right on the mouth."

"What the hell, Sis?"

"Well come on, will you do it, Tya" Rhiana asked.

Five hundred dollars sounded phenomenal, but the thought of being bought made her feel sick."

"I don't sell myself," Tya ground out.

"Oh, bugger that, I'm not asking you to sell your body. Just one kiss. Please?"

"Rhiana, cut it out you're embarrassing the poor woman," Blake growled.

Tya glanced at the people milling around and spied two women heading in their direction a petite brunette and a taller raven-haired woman who looked familiar. She glanced at Rhiana and guessed they were related. She wondered why their appearance had caused such angst. Puzzled, she turned back to her hunky eye candy. He stared at the approaching women looking thoroughly traumatized and ready to flee.

"I'll do it for nothing," Tya said as she pushed through between the tables. Endeva arrived at that moment in a swirl of gypsy skirts and disapproving tut tutting.

Tya made a hopping leap to Blake's side and slipped her bare arm around his waist. The heat from his body immediately seared her skin, his scent swirling around them.

She had never been so brazen before, but she didn't care. She had craved a kiss from this man from the moment she had tumbled into his arms.

"Look, I don't think..." Blake stuttered, turning to Tya.

She threw her arms around his neck and stood on tiptoe.

He looked down at her. The blue of her eyes seemed almost lavender with their fractured shadows and highlights. He glanced over his shoulder. The two women advanced determination etched on their faces.

He knew in that moment he needed distance, a barrier between him and Stephanie—between him, and his pain. Her unexpected appearance had caught him neither ready, nor prepared to deal with her wrath. With reckless speed he gathered what remnants of composure he had left.

"Oh, what the heck," he muttered turning to Tya. "Excuse me, but I'm about to ravish you, all in the aid of my emotional survival. Please don't slap me when I'm done, it will spoil the effect."

Tya giggled and stretched up to him, pressing her body against the hardness of his. "Well, ravish away."

Her breath brushed warm on his cheeks, a rich mixture of coffee and chocolate. Sensation zapped through him as his lips touched hers, softly, tentatively at first. Then he cupped her buttocks with both hands and pulled her against him. She came willingly. He slid his hand up behind her head and as he cradled it, he pressed hard, explored more deeply, his lips a sensual massage—a dance of skin on skin that left a trailing blaze of heat. His taste mixed with hers. Heat raced through him.

A soft moan escaped against his mouth.

"Blake." A woman's voice rose strident above the noise of the crowd.

The sound shivered down his spine. Memories bounded into his mind shattering his closeness to Tya. His first instinct was to pull away. Guilt shuddered through him as if he owed his jilted bride some sort of loyalty. He willed his mind to calm and stilled his body against the woman he held.

With a lingering caress he broke the contact even as he struggled for air, and equilibrium. Unwilling to let Tya go he held her pressed against him as he turned. "Hi Steph, fancy meeting you here."

She emerged from the crowd. His breath caught in his throat and his knees weakened as he gulped, trying to shut his gaping mouth. *My God, she was pregnant. Heavily pregnant.*

The woman held her hands out. "No one told me you were back."

Blake squeezed Tya hard against him sighing with relief when Stephanie stopped moving toward him.

"And no one told me you were pregnant." His words scraped out of his constricted throat.

She stroked her swelling belly barely covered by her t-shirt. "Bullshit, Blake. You knew we were pregnant when you left me standing at the altar."

Her words belted into him. He gasped for air. "Liar."

She glared at him. "Prove it."

Talisha stepped forward. "How can you just stand there and besmirch your reputation even more. I'm ashamed to call you my brother."

"Shut up Talisha, this is not your business." He glared at her trying to stop his gut from churning and to hold himself on the spot. He stared at his ex-fiancés baby bump. He felt repulsed, but at the same time attracted. It could be his child. Probably was his child. Oh hell, what did he do now?

"She's the only one whose supported me, Blake, when you did a cowardly runner, so she's entitled. More than four months of silence. You could have at least called, explained, apologized. anything."

"I had nothing to say to you Stephanie."

"But our baby? Surely you had thoughts about us, our baby, what you did?"

He flashed daggers in her direction. "One can't have thoughts about what one does not know."

Stephanie glared at him and shrugged. "Regardless, you're back now and in time for the birth. Please Blake say you'll be there for us." She stroked her baby bump.

Nausea washed over him made all the bitter by the confusion, hurt and guilt that jarred through him.

Stephanie stepped closer. "Come on Blake what you did was despicable, but you can make amends. Not that you have started off on the right foot by not telling me you were coming home. But I'm prepared to give you leeway because your father is so ill, but you owed me at least a call and an explanation."

He shook his head to negate her expectations.

"Don't be so mean Blake. Don't tell me your feelings are so changed. My feelings for you haven't changed, and I am ready to forgive you for abandoning me at the altar. Surely you haven't moved on." She pointed at Tya. "To the point we have no chance to make this right."

Tya extracted herself from Blake's embrace uneasy at the situation being played out in front of her.

He let her go. "There is no chance to make this right Stephanie. I don't love you anymore." He could barely articulate the words as he stared at the baby bump.

"But, Blake, I still love you and we're having a child." She stroked her belly again. "I want us to be a family."

If her words had been scorpions he would already be writhing in pain from their stings. He knew his love for this woman had died. For the first time since he saw her shagging Connor, he was free. Lightness washed through him. The world suddenly looked brighter even under the shadow of her pregnancy.

He shook his head. "We have no future, Stephanie. I don't love you anymore. As for your pregnancy it does not change how I feel about you." It did. It changed everything except for the fact his love for this woman was dead.

Talisha came to stand by Stephanie, clasping her arm in support. "Blake how can you be such a low life. I never thought you could do worse than the day you jilted her. You're a bastard. She's having your baby for Christ's sake."

Rhiana turned to her brother. "Yes, Blake how can you be so callous? I never thought you would be so heartless and uncaring."

He turned on Rhiana. "So, you knew about this?" He pointed to Stephanie's baby bump.

Rhiana shook her head. "No Blake I didn't know until right now. My sister failed to inform me."

Stephanie pulled away from Talisha's grip and stepped toward Blake. "You ran away once, but not this time. You have to take your responsibilities seriously."

"I do take my responsibilities very seriously, Stephanie, but you aren't one of them."

The woman's face colored a mottled pink. "What about our child, it's a boy, by the way. You are going to take responsibility for him, despite being preoccupied with adding more notches to your belt? What about me, his mother? You ran out on me, Blake. You owe me an explanation. No wait, you owe me a marriage—the life you promised me."

Blake glared back at Stephanie. "I owe you nothing, except maybe child support—*if* the child is mine."

Stephanie expression collapsed into a mask of anguish and fury. She charged at Blake beating against his chest with her fists. "How dare you. You bastard. You left me at the altar. Left me to bear your son, alone. No explanation, no justification. And you have the gall to question his parentage."

"Blake!" Talisha's screech made by standers turn and stare.

Blake fended off Stephanie's furious blows with firm but non aggressive blocks with his arms even as he retreated.

She followed, beating at his arms, chest and face.

"Stephanie stop. This is not the way to deal with him." Talisha tried to pull Stephanie back, but she shrugged her off.

Backed up against the trestle Blake finally grabbed her flailing arms and held them at her side. "Stop it, Stephanie. You're making a spectacle of yourself, and your agitation won't do the baby any good. This is not the place or time to address this issue." His words were measured, quiet, and firm. The slightest tremor roughed his tone. His face had paled, but his eyes flashed sparks and his mouth was drawn into a thin line.

Tya wondered if it was anger or anguish. She was struggling to comprehend the scene before her. A good looker but not much of a man to leave a woman pregnant at the altar. She sidled further away from him.

Stephanie pulled away.

Blake let her go but kept his arms up ready to restrain her again. Trying to steady his breathing and control the churning of his gut.

Tears streamed down her cheeks. "You bastard, Blake Gifford. Be in my office first thing Monday morning or I'll make life so difficult you'll wish you never came back."

Blake grimaced. "I already wish I hadn't come back. If it wasn't for my father's brush with death I wouldn't have."

"Bastard. Coward..."

"Enough of the theatrics, Stephanie. I'll be in your office Monday morning, and we *will* address the issues."

Talisha glance was full of daggers and her mouth curled up in a sneer. "And I called you brother."

Stephanie glared at him then turned on her heel and stomped away leaving Talisha trailing behind her.

"Holy shit." Blake sagged onto the edge of the trestle and covered his face with his hands.

Rhiana tottered forward and put her hand on his shoulder. "Blake."

He dropped his hands and looked at his sister. "Well, that went well."

"And the baby? Did she tell you?"

He shook his head. "No, she did not tell me."

"Even so it was a bit harsh saying it wasn't yours. Who else's would it be?"

Blake shook his head. "Look it probably is mine, but I have good reason to have doubts."

"Why?"

During the altercation his hair had escaped from its restraint and now tumbled onto his shoulders. He flicked it back impatiently with a trembling hand. Tremors shuddered through him and nausea roiled in his gut but he dredged up a smile. "I don't want to discuss it right now."

"Come on I think you need to go home." Rhiana picked up the zucchini's and handed them to her brother. "See you next week Tya. Thanks for helping."

Tya smiled vaguely and watched them go. His shapely backside tightly encased in his stained shorts, long legs pumping in brisk strides. A wave of disappointment wafted over her. It had been a long time since she had been kissed and never as delightfully as that. Her lips still tingled from his touch and his taste had invaded her mouth and somehow smeared itself across her heart. Even knowing she was not a good prospect for any man she unwisely yearned for some more of the troubled Blake Gifford. The mixture of confident, cheeky, and very sexy with a desperate vulnerability intrigued her. Whatever the hurt he'd experienced had left an indelible scar on his psyche.

***

Without any discussion with his sister, Blake took the driver's seat.

Rhiana didn't protest.

With concentrated precision he negotiated the crowded car park. His search for healing and new love had occasionally gotten him into corners and beds he had quickly wanted to extract himself from when he realized lust had misdirected him into the arms of that particular female. His little sister was probably right on the money when she said he needed help. This morning's encounter had stirred up a maelstrom of emotions. *Was the baby his? She said she told him. Why lie. The only thing he was sure of was that he no longer loved Stephanie. And that itself made things more complicated now there was a child to consider.*

They drove home in silence, but from time-to-time Blake could feel Rhiana's gaze on him. He sensed her concern but couldn't reassure her and didn't want to discuss it. He needed time to process the revelations.

As they entered the house, his stepmother called from the kitchen. "Breakfast you two, or did you grab something at the market?"

"Mum, they had nothing fit for my body so we're both starving. If you're making pancakes, I'm sure Blake will eat a few. I bought lemons and some organic strawberry jam and some local honey."

"Yes thanks, Alice, three or four should fill the hole," Blake said as he dumped the bags of produce on the counter knowing full well he had no appetite. Apprehension curled in his gut at what was to come. He poured himself a glass of the organic apple juice his sister had just opened then sat at the table to flick through the Sunday paper.

He could hear Rhiana whispering to Alice.

Alice shushed her and went to collect her husband.

When his father was settled Rhiana whispered again in Alice's ear.

Blake didn't bother to look up. "Go ahead, Rhiana, you might as well tell them. We saw Stephanie at the market and she's pregnant. And Blake had a meltdown."

"Blake, that is such an exaggeration," Rhiana protested.

Blake cleared his throat and looked up. "No, it's not, Rhiana. There's no point denying the unexpected encounter rattled me, even with the distraction."

"Well, it was a shock, and you handled it well, Blake."

"Bullshit. Let's face it, it was the last thing I expected, firstly to see Stephanie at the market and secondly, and more importantly, to discover she's pregnant. She says it's mine and to make it worse I'm not in love with her so there will be no reconciliation like she wants. Where the hell does that leave me?"

His father cleared his throat. "Blake, who's child would it be but yours? Did you know she was pregnant when you did a runner?"

Blake looked directly at his father. "No Dad I had no idea, but I figured she did. So why didn't she tell me if the kid is mine. Why hide it from me. Devious bitch."

"Blake that's a harsh assessment."

"Not really considering. But what am I going to do with the revelations who knows. My life is in tatters."

"You loved her. Will you go back to her now?"

Blake shook his head. "No, but it doesn't stop me feeling guilty about the child."

His dad's hand sat heavily on his shoulder. "You'll work it out son. Whatever you decide we will support you. Now let's eat before Alice's pancakes go cold."

Blake's appetite had shriveled under the examination of this morning's encounter, but he took three pancakes determined to put up a good front. But it was the grower of the strawberries that squashed sweet against his tongue that filled his thoughts, not Stephanie.

A clatter of heels brought a waft of malevolence into the room. Talisha barged through the door, slammed her handbag down on the bench and glared at Blake.

He forced himself to keep his expression blank. Unease trickled over his skin. This would be a defining moment. He glanced around the room wondering if the others actually felt the same as Talisha appeared to but were well mannered enough to hide it.

Talisha flicked her short dark bob behind her ears, placed both hands on the bench and leaned toward him. "How can you even dare show your face back here? Do you think everyone is going to forget what you did? I'm ashamed to be associated with such a gutless bastard. What sort of *man* leaves his pregnant bride standing at the altar?"

"Talisha, stop. Muir is in no condition to deal with theatrics right now." Alice held up her hand to ward her older daughter off.

Talisha frowned. "No, he isn't, and Blake's to blame. All the shame, innuendo and incriminations brought his heart attack on." She pointed her finger at Blake.

The long red varnished nail drew Blake's focus as he avoided meeting his sister's glare.

"Stress brought Dad down and you caused it."

Blake reared back at the venom in his stepsister's voice.

"Talisha, that's not fair. Muir had health issues before Blake's problems," Alice protested.

Blake glanced at Alice then back at Talisha. This time he looked directly into her eyes determined not to be brow beaten. Nausea swished in his gut. He sat taller. "If that's how you feel let's have this out right now—once and for all. There is no point skulking around the subject."

"Exactly—time for you to face the music. To take your responsibilities seriously. It's disgusting the way you ran away without a word of explanation or apology."

"Talisha, no," his father growled.

"It needs to be said, Dad. If you can't or won't do it, I can and will."

Blake glanced around the expectant faces. "A lot needs to be said, Talisha, including the truth."

Talisha glowered at him. "There's nothing that can clear you, Blake. The truth is, you left your pregnant bride at the altar and ran off. In a few weeks she's going to be a single mum raising your kid."

"Really!" The word exploded from him taking the air in his lungs with it. He tried to draw breath. His lungs rebelled. He gasped, coughed and gasped again. Precious air filtered in. "I didn't know she was pregnant until this morning."

"Bit shocked are we then? Stephanie says she told you. You knew before the wedding."

Silence descended cold and accusing.

Blake glanced around at the others.

"Talisha." One word, full of admonishment whispered out of his father.

Sweat beaded on Blake's forehead, nausea swirled in his gut. All he could see in his mind was Stephanie on her back with her wedding gown hitched up moaning in pleasure as Connor thrust into her.

He tried to unclench his jaw, but in the end only managed to squeeze the bitter words out between his teeth. "She'll have to prove it's mine."

"Blake," his father yelped.

"I beg your pardon. She has to prove the child's yours," Talisha screeched.

"Yes, she'll have to prove it." Rage exploded in him. *So, this is what they think—that I abandoned my pregnant bride at the altar. I can see it in their faces. They're all waiting for me to make it right. To justify my cowardly actions. Well here goes.*

Better late than never to deliver a few home truths for his family and anyone else who would listen. Blake realized the real depth of his mistake for the first time. He should have stayed and exposed his bride's cheating instead of slinking off with his tail between his legs.

Talisha's face flushed red. She clenched her fists. "My God, Blake is there no end to your shameless behavior. To deny...to accuse. How dare you?"

"I dare, dear sister, because I saw her shagging Connor less than an hour before the ceremony. To me that indicates there could be some question over who fathered her child. It could be his, or it could be mine or anyone else's for that matter."

"You lying bastard. How dare you say such things?'

"I dare because it's true." Blake looked from one to the other.

His father's face had paled, and Blake flinched with concern about the damage his revelations would cause to his health.

He looked at Alice.

The faintest of smiles curved her mouth. She nodded to him.

Blake felt an unexpected alien warmth radiating from his stepmother for the first time. She at least believed him.

Sweat beaded on his father's forehead. "You have proof of her indiscretion?"

Blake nodded.

"Well, there you go. I knew there would be a good reason," Rhiana squawked.

"I'm not going to stand here and have you besmirch Stephanie in that way," Talisha shouted.

The room wavered. Blake gulped. *This is it. My one chance at redemption.* He coughed.

Alice handed him a glass of water.

He sipped the liquid and swallowed. He didn't know what to think. Of course, he could have fathered the child. *But Stephanie pregnant? Holy shit what a bloody mess.*

Despite his shock he determined not to be pilloried by Talisha. He would not take all the blame this time. He pulled out his phone and held it out to Talisha. "I have proof. Do you want to see for yourself?"

"Blake."

The censure in his father's wavering voice fueled his anger, but he knew the law.

Talisha paled and stepped back. She shook her head. "Liar."

"So, you'll not take my word for it?" he said placing the phone with delicate precision on the table. It sat there, still and silent, like a viper ready to strike. He glared at those around him.

"She told you Blake. Was that why you left?"

"No Talisha, Stephanie did not tell me. I left because she was having it off with my best mate. What did you expect me to do – just go ahead and marry her with my mate's cum still warm inside her."

"Eww, that's disgusting Blake."

He glanced at his little sister then turned back to Talisha.

"Liar. Now you're back you must face the music."

Blake shook his head. "I wouldn't have come back at all except for Dad, and I definitely wouldn't have come back for her."

"You will have to take your responsibilities seriously. It's your son. He deserves a family. Just because you're a chicken-livered commitment phobic he shouldn't have to suffer."

He glared at Talisha. "I am perfectly capable of doing what is required. Thanks so much for the benefit of doubt, Sis."

Talisha glared back at him. "Maybe if you had been man enough to do the right thing you might have got a better welcome."

"I'll do the right thing, Talisha, *if* the child proves to be mine."

"Of course, it's yours. Regardless of your scandalous claim I know Stephanie would never be unfaithful."

"There is no 'of course' about it."

"Bastard," Talisha snatched up her handbag and clattered from the room. "I'm not coming back until he goes."

Blake looked at his father.

He sat pale but composed.

Rhiana now stood by Alice. "We believe you, Blake. Never did take to Stephanie—too ruthless for me."

Blake grinned; a tiny tickle of satisfaction at finally having the whole wretched episode out in the open softened his uncertainty at being home. "So now you know."

"You should have confronted her at the time, Blake."

"I know that now, Dad, but I was shattered. Seeing them, going at it, hammer and tongs her wedding gown just hitched up for Christ's sake."

"Eww." Rhiana screwed her face up. "I always thought Stephanie was a bit of a bitch."

"I didn't know she was pregnant. What a bloody mess."

His father patted his shoulder. "One step at a time, Blake, we can sort this out."

Blake nodded to his father as he put his mug down. He guessed his father would want to talk these revelations through. The desire to flee whipped over him as shock at the suddenness of the confrontation tingled over him.

In the vain hope of delaying further discussion he looked to his stepmother. "Shall I do the dishes, Alice, before Dad sequesters me in the office for the rest of the afternoon?"

Alice flicked the tea towel she held in his direction. "Off with you, Blake. Your father has been waiting ever so patiently to talk to you. There will be plenty of other times for you to do the dishes. No point in delaying the inevitable. You'll both feel better for getting it off your chest. And Blake, whatever happens I'm in your corner."

Blake nodded. "Thanks Alice. I should have appreciated you more all these years."

Alice smiled. "We've got by Blake."

Dismissed, and pleased with having finally made his peace with his stepmother Blake pushed his father to the office.

He helped his father move to the comfortable recliner and settle back in the deep leather chair. Blake raised the footrest and placed a throw over him. It cut deep into Blake's heart to see his father so grey and haggard and looking so very tired. He knew his drama did not help. Guilt stabbed as he felt the net close around him.

He sat on the edge of the chair opposite. "Dad, I'm sorry. I know you don't need this right now, but I didn't know..."

"Well now you do, you'll have to take responsibility—if it's yours."

Blake looked directly at his father. "I don't know. I suppose it is. I did not even think Stephanie was capable of being unfaithful. God, I loved her...we were good together."

"Even when she chose to take up a position with Hector and Hector instead of joining you in your firm. Alice, and I, both sensed you were disappointed."

Blake shrugged. "We had our moments and yes, I was bitterly disappointed. Perhaps I wasn't 'man' enough, ruthless enough for her, but then why choose Connor."

"It's possible. She's a very ambitious woman. Do you still love her?"

Blake slouched back into the deepness of the chair. It cradled him. "No, of that, I'm sure. The only thing I am sure of at the moment to be honest now the shock has worn off."

"I'm not sorry you feel that way but for the future it's important to see if this baby is yours."

"The child changes it all—if its mine."

"No, it doesn't. You can be a father without being husband to the mother. Please don't consider that option, because you'll regret it."

"Yes, I suppose so."

"Listen to me, Blake. You cannot make that sacrifice if you no longer care for Stephanie."

"All right, I'm listening. So, what do we do now?"

"Are you sure you want to do this. It could have ramifications you've not thought of."

"I need to know."

"Right then let's get Lyall onto it. It's better if it comes from a neutral person, I think. Do you know when she's due?"

Blake shook his head

Blake felt more at ease now than he had for a long time. He'd do the right thing by the child if it proved to be his. But what would be the right thing—money, time. Of course, the best thing was to form a family but he couldn't do that knowing he had no feelings for Stephanie. His gut clenched as if he'd been kicked. He struggled with a multitude of emotions—hurt, betrayal, anger, but looming largest, was the sense of being trapped. He had once loved her with a passion beyond reason. She had been the only one for him. It had terrified him that feelings would still be there and yet he mourned the thought of such a great love dying a final death. *I'm a bloody fool.*

His father's voice broke through his tumultuous thoughts. "I need my rest, Blake, but before you go, these came in before my heart attack. The new guy in the accounts department noticed and he seemed a bit concerned. He brought them to me." His father held out several water bills. "These are for the property at thirty five Thistle Street,"

"There's a problem?" Blake asked a sliver of irritation brushing over his skin.

"Well sort of. These bills seem excessive... for a disused residential block."

Blake frowned as he took the invoices. He started back. "Bloody hell, this is enough water to fill several swimming pools—large ones at that."

"Have you given any thought to selling the land? Closing that chapter of your life?"

"No. Mum's ashes are there. I won't let someone build over them."

His father sighed. "No. I suppose not."

He sensed his reply had frustrated his father.

"Then you might need to take care of it, son. It is probably a broken pipe or something."

"I will, Dad. Now get some rest."

CHAPTER 4

As the soft light of dawn filtered into his room Blake rubbed his scratchy eyes. He flopped over in the bed for the hundredth time. The bedclothes had wrapped around his torso like a tight bandage. Blake snatched at them dragging them loose and shoving them onto the floor. He laid on his back staring at the ceiling. His gut churned at the thought of the inevitable confrontation ahead.

He dragged his aching body off the bed and stood for a long time under the stinging hot water of the shower. He dressed in his best suit and favorite shirt trying to bolster his courage. It would be best to get this issue off his back early then he might be able to make a few decisions about his future.

The offices of Hector, Hector and Huxtable located in town provided staff parking only and Blake had trouble finding a park. Feeling hot and bothered, he stepped out of the lift on the fourth floor fully appreciating the air-conditioning.

The receptionist took his name and called it through to Stephanie.

Blake barely got seated when Stephanie appeared from her office and sashayed across the room. She smiled. Tall, lissome, full bosomed with glowing skin and long dark hair swirled up in a bun. Impeccable and sexy despite her pregnancy in her three-piece suit and six-inch heels. His inner male instantly responded to her sensual strut toward him. They had sizzled together in bed. Blake mentally slammed a door on his memories letting his humiliation at her hands provide a solid seal.

"Blake, nice that you actually managed to get here. I thought you might have skipped town again."

Her bitter sarcasm left him gasping. Didn't she have any guilt? Obviously, she intended to play her innocence right to the end.

"I said I would be here."

She frowned and tapped one red vanished fingernail against the sleeve of his suit jacket.

"I couldn't be sure. Just a few months ago you said you'd be at the altar too."

Blake flinched inwardly at her touch, but didn't move his arm determined to hide his response. He shrugged his shoulders. "Some things can't be helped."

"Of all the bastards..."

"You want to play this out in public?"

She shook her head.

Blake indicated for her to lead the way. He had absolutely no intention of playing his mess out in front of the receptionist or anyone else who might appear.

Stephanie took his cue and waltzed up the passage.

Her swaying buttocks encased in a clinging skirt and shapely calves held his attention. He still found her physically attractive, bloody hell, but at the same time the urge to strangle her teased him.

As he entered her office, she stopped short and held the door wide. Her perfume wafted over him, the same perfume she had always worn, cloying and sweet. He could feel the heat from her body as she thrust her baby bump and ample cleavage right under his nose. He stepped aside.

She sighed and pranced to her desk. A pout had replaced the pinned on practiced smile. She indicated a seat.

Blake slipped into it, sitting stiffly. He wanted this meeting over.

"We need to talk about the child."

"I'm calling him Stephen."

"After his mother, I see."

"What's wrong with that considering his father had gone AWOL."

"There is nothing wrong with it. Now, what are you expecting in regard to the baby...Stephen?"

Stephanie frowned. "Straight to business then?"

Blake nodded. "There is nothing else between us."

Stephanie scowled. "Really, Blake? An explanation would be appropriate in the circumstances. You did leave me at the altar."

Raged surge through him. "Do you really need an explanation, Stephanie?"

"I'm entitled to..."

"I have some papers here regarding your child once its born."

"What papers?"

"Talisha believes it's mine. I want to know for sure."

"Blake, darling, who else's would he be?"

Rage ignited in his gut. He stirred in his seat. "Connor's perhaps."

Her laughter tinkled around the office. "Whatever makes you think Stephen is Connor's?"

He sat in mesmerized stillness for a moment, unable to believe her audacity. He swallowed then pulled out his phone. It took only seconds to find the image he wanted. With the video playing on the screen he slid the device across the table. "This might explain it."

Stephanie picked up the phone and stared at the images flicking across the screen. The only color left in her face was her blushed cheeks and the crimson lips.

"You saw us? You knew?"

"Yes."

"And you didn't say."

"I was too shocked at the time, and after there seemed no point. I wanted to erase that scene, and you, from my mind."

"I'm sorry, Blake, I really am. It just happened."

"On the way to the wedding, God damn it. Wasn't I good enough in bed for you, or what?"

The color rushed back into her face. "No Blake. We *were* good together it's..."

"It's what? Wasn't I man enough, ruthless enough? Is that what you needed, a man willing to climb over bodies to get to the top at all costs? Is that what it was, my lack of ambition? Then why Connor? He's the least ambitious creature I know. A surf board and a wave about does it."

In the second of hesitation before she shook her head Blake saw a shadow of disappointment flutter before she blinked it away.

"I don't know, Blake. I loved you. Still love you. Can we get passed this? Start again. You, me, and our son."

She might as well have slapped him with a wet fish. He stared at her, unable to find the words to respond. He took a deep breath.

"No, Stephanie, my love for you died that day. Anyway, what about Connor?"

Stephanie waved her hand. "Connor was never in the picture. It was only ever you."

Blake shook his head, placed the papers on the table then stood up and retrieved his phone. "Too late. Besides, I'm in love with someone else."

Stephanie pouted. "Is that why you want to know about Stephen?"

"Not really. It seemed the right thing to do. I've demanded Connor be tested too. I want no loose ends."

"Well, despite your attitude, I'm not giving up on you, Blake. While you're single there is always a chance for me to win you back."

Blake looked her over. She was an attractive woman, intelligent, smart, capable and ruthless and untrustworthy. The last two negated all the others. "Don't waste your time. We're over. Get the tests done as soon as the baby arrives. Send me the bill."

"And if I don't want to?"

"Then I'll see you in court. I want this finished, now—clear cut, no rumors and innuendo, no questions."

"Blake, please don't be act this way. I love you."

"I don't want your sort of love." He turned and strode from the office gently pulling the door closed behind him.

But it wasn't finished. It might never be finished if the unborn baby Stephen proved to be his. The thought of continuing contact with Stephanie throughout the child's life weighed heavy over him like an impending thunderstorm. He feared she would never let him go. *Please don't be mine. Please. Poor kid, to be so unwanted.* Guilt tickled at him.

***

By the time he returned to the house he had managed to shut the guilt about the child away in a secure corner of his mind. The issue of the mother remained to haunt him.

"Have you delivered the papers, son."

"Yes, and as I predicted it made her mad as hell. A bit shocked when I showed her the video."

"Best you erase it now it's served its purpose."

"I will, Dad. I'm going to Thistle Street are you sure you don't want to come?"

His father shook his head. "No, Blake. I know it's the twentieth anniversary and her birthday but I can't bear to dredge up the memories. I'll stay away and remember her as she was."

"All right, Dad."

He understood his father's reluctance. There had been times when he wondered why he continued to visit the spot from time to time. It had been a few years now but even so he couldn't give it up.

The unlikely mistake that had his mother at the empty house still haunted him. They should have been at thirty-five Thistle Crescent, not thirty-five Thistle Street. The surprise birthday for his mother, Francis, he and his father so secretively planned had seemed a great idea at the time. How his mother and her close friend, Grace had ended up at the wrong house had never been established but the squatter in the recently emptied public housing didn't take kindly to their intrusion in his drug-induced madness. He had beaten them, and robbed them, before fleeing. Hours later their fate had been revealed shattering the Gifford and Mitton families forever.

Maddened by grief his father had purchased the derelict property, demolished it and built an eight-foot fence around the perimeter. Together they had buried her ashes and planted a rose on the spot of her death and placed a plaque by the base. His father had never visited the site again, but Blake had gone occasionally pruned the rose bush, fertilized it, and conferred with his mother. A lot less since he had been involved with Stephanie.

Blake parked and stared at the fence. He shivered, not sure if he could even get out the car. His heart fluttered erratically as memories flooded his mind, and he let them flow until the sharp edge of horror softened into nostalgic memories. He moved restlessly in his seat then climbed out of the car. He leaned on the bonnet and waited for his legs to stop trembling and his courage to awaken before he pushed upright and stalked across the road.

He pulled out the key, but the gate swung open under his initial touch. It had always been locked. He started back at first, surprised, then angry that someone had invaded her space.

A wall of green confronted him when he pushed the gate wide and stepped through the opening. Blake closed his eyes, shook his head then opened his eyes again. The garden remained in all its productive green glory. *What the bloody hell?*

He stood frozen staring at the mass of green plants that should not have been there. He reached out and rubbed a tomato leaf between his fingers. The tangy aroma tantalized his nostrils. Someone was growing tomatoes on his block. The sense of violation carried him forward with exaggerated strides. Rage seethed, cramping his lungs and filling his head. *I'll put a stop to this invasion right now.*

To the left of the gate, he found a narrow pathway between two towering crops of tomatoes. The plants rustled loudly as he brushed past

Bloody squatters, how dare they take over my land. Trespassers. I'll fix them. He returned to the gate and reached for his phone.

"Lucas, do you have a machine and driver free. Yes, right now. Thirty-five Thistle Street. Come up the back lane. I have a job for you."

An hour later, Lucas arrived with the bulldozer. The sun burnt down on Blake's head, but he didn't really notice. Rage heated him from the inside that strangers had violated his memories by taking over the block where his mother had been murdered and her ashes were interred.

Lucas climbed down and helped Blake open the double back gates.

"What's this about, mate?" he asked.

"Some cheeky bastards have taken over this block of mine to grow veggies. Been using my water for quite a while."

"Wow." Lucas stood and stared at the lush garden. "Feed an army with that lot. Heard they do it a lot in the eastern seaboard. Guerilla gardeners taking over vacant blocks to feed the poor."

"Damn it, Lucas. They're not feeding anyone because I'm going to flatten it."

"Blake, ease up mate. It's only a garden and you can afford the water."

"Don't tell me to ease up. The bastards are violating my mother's memory."

Lucas frowned at him. "I think it is better than the scrubby wasteland here before."

"That's for me to decide, Lucas, not some bloody strangers making a buck out of my loss."

"Fine, if that's what you want." Lucas climbed up into the cab and started the machine. It growled and ground metal on metal as it moved towards the crops in a cloud of foul smelling diesel.

Blake stood back and watched.

Bellows of protests rose above the growl of the machine. An older man emerged from the lush greenery. "Stop. Bloody hell, stop. What the hell are you doing?" He waved the hoe. "What're you doing in here—this is private property."

Blake waved for Lucas to halt and cut the engine. A deep silence encompassed them.

"Yes, it is—mine," Blake replied. "Your occupation of my land ends now. Get out of the way."

The old man's mouth gaped open. He shook his head and snapped his mouth shut. He placed the other hand on the hoe handle and took two steps back. "Jordan, get here," he shouted. "We have trouble."

Blake held out his hands in a placating gesture. "It's all right, mate, I'm not about to attack you. If you leave peacefully that will be the end of it."

He heard heavy feet thudding towards them in a jumbled tattoo.

Blake glanced over his shoulder but couldn't see anyone through the plants. He turned back to the man.

"Oh—well I suppose it had to happen sometime," the man said still holding the hoe in a defensive stance.

A younger man burst out of the narrow gap between the corn and tomatoes. He had come armed with a shovel while a second older one following him had his fists up and clenched.

"What ya doing here, mate? Back off. If you want food, we'll give you as much as you need. No need for violence." the younger man shouted.

Blake held his hands up and backed up until he pressed against the tomato bushes. "Gentlemen, I'm not looking for trouble. All I want is for you to get out of the way. I intend clearing my land."

"Hey guys, sorry I'm late."

The honeyed tones danced across him. Blake turned and stared intently down the narrow path. Her. *By God, it's her.*

Tya appeared—scruffy denim shorts and a cut off tee leaving her long shapely legs and midriff bare, a glittering jewel nestled in her navel. He bought his gaze to her face with its delicate heart shape topped by white blonde spiky hair.

Tya froze.

He saw her throat move as she swallowed a number of times.

The pink tip of her tongue raced across her lips. "What are you doing here? How did you find me?"

Blake pushed himself upright. A multitude of emotions tumbled through him, but the shock of having her right in front of him diluted his rage. "I wasn't looking for you. I've come to re-claim what's mine."

Tya stopped, cane basket swinging slightly in her hand. She stared at him, her eyes wide and troubled, her mouth drawn into a thin line, a deep frown marring her high forehead. "Excuse me?"

"I said, I've come to re-claim what's mine—this block."

"Errrr... this is your block of land?"

"Yes, it is. You've just taken it over?"

"Ummm, yes. You haven't been near the place for ages. People are going hungry, I thought..."

"You thought, did you? Are you in the habit of taking over un-used land?"

"Well yes, actually, my friends and I..."

Blake moved toward her.

She took a step back.

He stepped closer.

She stood taller, lifting her chin in a defiant gesture and looked at him with an unblinking stare.

"You had no bloody right to come in here, to take possession of my land and do this."

Tya slapped her hands on her hips and glared at him. "The garden hasn't hurt it, it's all still here, every square inch of dirt and more. You can have it back—as soon as the crops are finished."

Blake absorbed her words. His tongue twisted around the words he thought he should say, but they wouldn't form. *I can have it back—when the crops are finished. Bloody hell, the cheek of her.*

"You charged me, well my sister, for vegetables grown with my water. The bloody cheek of it. You charged me. You're making money off my hard labor. My personal effort."

"Well, I didn't know, did I?

"Well maybe you didn't, but you were all over me quick enough."

"It wasn't just me if I remember rightly. You just wanted to shock that Stephanie woman."

"That had nothing to do with this."

"What's your problem then?"

"I don't want this land used."

"Why? What's so special about it?"

"It's a memorial to my mother."

"And?"

Someone snickered behind her.

His indignation exploded and he glared at the younger lad. "Her ashes are buried here. You can't grow vegetables on her ashes."

The older woman who had been at the market with Tya came up to stand behind the blonde firebrand.

"I want you lot gone, now. I'm not waiting for the crops to be finished. And you better not come back."

Blake waved Lucas forward. "Get it done, Lucas."

Lucas started the machine.

Tya stepped forward until her toes touched the sharp edge of the blade. "We don't *make* money. All except the excess is given to battling families and the women's shelter. Tya waved to encompass the four. We, all of us, get nothing except some veggies and a donation to the defibrillator charity and we have receipts."

"Bullshit. I saw you selling the produce. Bet you make a mint. Get on with it, Lucas."

His mate cut the engine, climbed down of the machine and came to stand beside him. "Nah, mate. Here are the keys if you want to do it. I'm not squashing some bird and her vegetables. She's doing a good thing. Count me out."

Blake took the keys. He glared at his mate then stomped to the machine. As he settled in the seat he realized Tya had not moved. *Bloody fool. Beautiful, stubborn, God damn sexy little fool.*

The others had moved aside.

He started the engine. The big machine rumbled and grunted.

Tya stood unmoving.

Blast it woman, get out of my way.

"You will have to run me over. I'm not moving," she shouted.

Her feisty stance and provocative words beat at him. Her breasts pushed against the tee, her torso smooth and golden, carved in shapely curves. Below the ragged edge of her shorts, she held her long tanned legs stiffly straight, feet wide apart.

Something ignited in his chest. His heart jumped and bounced. He crashed the gears into place and gunned the engine.

Tya stood tall.

He stared at the woman in front of him with her toes almost touching the metal of the blade—petite, blonde, and looking very vulnerable despite the flashing blue eyes and her wide full mouth screaming words of retribution and warning.

A sliver of emotion sliced into him. His heart skipped a beat then raced—fast and furious. He couldn't breathe as he stared at her. With a hasty flick of his tongue he wet his dry lips and gasped little hisses of air into his paralyzed lungs. His stomach somersaulted and his clenched fist trembled on the gears. They rattled metallically. He held the steering wheel so tightly his other hand cramped. With steely determination he uncurled his fingers and reached blindly down to set the machine in motion.

Tya continued to scream at him.

He watched her.

Like a mad woman she abused him. Her white blonde hair flicking from side to side into confused disarray and tears formed glistening trails down her rosy cheeks. She shook her fist at him releasing a clod of wet earth. It landed with a splat on the windscreen. Another quickly followed.

Blake sat mesmerized by her beauty, her spirit, and her rage. His heart imploded into a fiery ball. Awareness hit him with shattering clarity. This woman, one he barely knew, had smashed the wall enclosing his heart letting tendrils of emotion wind around it out of control and stubbornly unbidden. The icy protective layer disintegrated into a puddle of warmth and tenderness. Denial grabbed at him, stoking his rage.

"Here, Tya, wash him away with this," Endeva yelled as she flicked the hose across the gap between them.

Tya grabbed it up. She aimed it at Blake. A stream of water shot out of the hose and splattered against the short windscreen.

Blake ducked. *Holy shit she intends to drown me.* Another stream hurtled towards him catching him in the shoulder. His backside slid on the wet seat. He grabbed the steering wheel to stay seated. *Well if she wants war then she's got it.*

He wiped his face then set the machine in motion. Every fiber of his being cried out for him to stop as a maelstrom of emotions strangled his heart.

The machine lumbered forward.

Another gush of water flattened itself against the windscreen and at the last moment she stepped to the side.

"Damn you to hell, Blake Gifford. Take that." Tya screamed, blasting with the full force of the stream of water.

The blast stung his shoulder. "Owww," he yelled.

Another blast caught him in the chest tearing his shirt buttons apart. He gasped as the needles of water stung his skin. He looked down at his foe as the machine ground slowly passed. It crunched and ground as it demolished the edge of the sweet corn bed. The tall stalks of corn rustled and cracked as the shovel ripped through the edge of the bed and swept forward tearing the roots out of the ground and crushing the golden stems and green leaves into the rich dark earth.

She held the hose like a weapon as she came right up by the machine's tracks and applied the full force of the water.

"Damn you, Blake Gifford. How can you do this? Destroy good food. Food to feed Aussie battlers."

As she stood there the epitome of a modern apocalyptic warrior woman something sparked in his soul. A flicker of admiration, awareness perhaps, whatever the cause his heart melted under the heat it generated. Confusion swamped him. She was beautiful, sexy, and very desirable but it was more than lust that stirred within him. He knew lust, often, and this wasn't it. He couldn't identify it. The thought of identifying it terrified him. Irritated with it weakening his anger he pushed the sensation away desperately summoning his anger to squash it into oblivion. But it wouldn't come.

The rage that drove him melted away leaving him trembling with the thrill of desire—heart and soul longing. He suddenly wanted this woman in a way he had never wanted a woman before. The thrill of desire and pulses of emotion annihilated his lack of trust even as he wrestled with seething fury because she had penetrated his defenses. He caved under his craving to embrace and kiss her until she melted to putty in his hands gripped him.

How had this particular woman demolished the wall he had erected and touched his heart and invaded his soul so easily?

He took exception to this foreign emotion intruding into the coldness inside him because he didn't want her getting under his skin, in his head and capturing his heart. Resentment surged at the way she reached out to him with her sparkling blue eyes, wide pouting mouth, wild untamed spirit, and the delicate feminine aura that flowed around her.

But her laugh caressed his hearing, made sweet music in his ears and her perfume sent a whirlpool of hunger swirling all the way through his gut, hardening his cock and yet calming him, taming his inner male bringing forth the need to protect and worship her. He tried to deny the attraction. To brush it away, but she remained firmly lodged in his mind, in his heart, and in his dreams, unbidden.

He cut the engine and climbed down under the barrage of stinging water.

"Stop drowning me, Tya. I've stopped. You've won, okay."

She ignored him or perhaps didn't hear him and kept the hose directed at him.

He put his hands up to protect his face and strode towards her.

"Stop. Turn the water off, Tya. You've won."

She hesitated.

Then the stream of water eased, and Blake bounced forward and closed the gap. He grabbed her shoulders even as she brought the hose up again.

"Stop, Tya, the garden is yours."

She stared up at him the hose now hanging loosely in her hands.

Blake stared down at her. Their feet sank in the oozing muddy ground chewed up by the bulldozer. Tension swirled around them. Awareness exploded in him, leaving him vulnerable. His breathing jerked in his chest and his knees weakened.

"My God, Tya. I'm sorry. I..."

The magnetism of her sexual aura drew him toward her. He could feel her call, a primitive out of control call of pure lust and yet ardor, attraction and a gentleness he couldn't resist softened the edges. From a blazing hell fire woman protecting the fruits of her labor, to a blazing hell fire woman igniting his passion.

He stared down into her eyes. They darkened. He slid into the shimmering depths of the tear-filled orbs.

She closed her lids as he drew closer.

Her flowery scent had almost been annihilated by mud and water but her natural aroma called to him. He touched her mouth, tentatively at first, then pulled her against him and plundered her mouth with a ruthless need. He demanded a response, and it came.

Desperate, wild, and passionate, yet vulnerable, as she trembled against his hardness. Nothing mattered but the two of them standing in the mud with the wreckage of the garden beside them and a new hope in their hearts.

Her heart thudded behind her breast as he held her against his soaking wet chest. Every inch of his skin tingled, all the hair stood on end at her nearness. The roughness of her wet t-shirt rubbed against his chest, stoking the fire inside.

Overwhelmed and breathless under a tsunami of emotion Blake finally pulled away. He stared down at her lips, now swollen and moist from his plunder.

The thoughts in his mind circled into a whirlpool and fled as he opened his mouth to speak. He shut his mouth and stared at his antagonist. He took a deep slow breath in. 'Tya, I'm sorry. For being so angry... so angry about a lot of things."

She reached up and trailed her fingers over his mouth.

They left a searing path on the tender skin.

"You do something to me, Blake Gifford, when you kiss me and it's very dangerous."

"I'm not dangerous, Tya."

She nodded. "Oh, yes you are—very dangerous."

"Why, Tya."

"Never mind. Can we keep the garden forever?"

"We'll see. Perhaps we could discuss it over dinner."

She shook her head. "I don't do dinner."

"Come on, Tya, surely you owe me that. You are, after all, getting free run of my land and free water. We could discuss terms in a civilized manner over dinner."

She smiled.

That small tendril of emotion vibrated inside his chest.

Tya shrugged. "I suppose if you put it that way."

"Good. Tomorrow night then?"

"All right, Blake, you win. I'll have dinner with you tomorrow night—business only."

The tinge of regret in her tone bothered him. She had agreed only out of obligation. He desperately needed her to want to come. For the first time for a long time a tingle of excitement about being with a woman buzzed through him. Much more than lust.

Embarrassment edged in. He floundered under the emotion sweeping through him. Cringing inwardly at the outburst of rage that had driven him to such extremes. Shame beat at him as he glanced at the destruction left in its wake.

Disapproval emanated from the four other gardeners.

Why had he let his old grief, Stephanie's treachery and shocking disclosure drive him crazy? To turn him into an irrational idiot who acts first and thinks after—with remorse.

The bulldozer still sat in the middle of the corn crop.

He held his hands out. "I'm so sorry. I should never have done this. Please forgive me, Tya?"

She shook her head. "I don't know if I can, but I suppose you had the right. It is your land."

"That does not excuse my behavior..."

She held her hands in surrender. "It's done now, Blake. Please take your bulldozer away so I can salvage as much as possible."

He nodded, climbed up into the machine and started the engine. Carefully, he reversed the machine out onto the back lane. He climbed down and called Lucas.

"Come back get your machine, I won't be needing it."
***

As the sound of the engine faded Endeva hurried up and grabbed Tya in a bear hug. "You did it, my girl. But why did you let him kiss you? You're setting yourself up for heartbreak with such foolishness."

"I don't know Endeva, it just seemed to happen."

"You sent him scampering off with his tail between his legs," Jordan said.

Tya sagged into Endeva's embrace barely able to stay upright on trembling legs. "I was so scared, but I couldn't let him destroy good food. Actually, I didn't think he would back down so easily."

"I would if I faced you, Tya," Jordan quipped.

"Yeah, me too. Hey girls, do you think he's something to do with the roses? Do you think he's connected to Francis? Perhaps we trespassed on something special for him?"

Tya pulled away from Endeva. Shivers of guilt whispered over her skin. "Yes, his mother's ashes are buried under the rose bush. If he comes back, I'll take him to see what we have done to his memorial."

"What now, Tya," Endeva asked.

Tya looked around the demolished garden. "We salvage the damaged corn then its business as usual. I don't think he's going to evict us any time soon.'

"This is good news."

"Yes, it is. I've agreed to have dinner with him—to discuss terms for the land usage."

"Do we plant the new sweet corn and tomatoes?"

"Yep. He said we could have use of the land indefinitely."

"Right then, I'll finish the watering, you fellas; see what you can do with the compost system before it gets too dark. Are you right with the corn, Tya?"

She nodded.

As the others dispersed into the gathering gloom she squatted down and began tearing the cobs from the crushed stalks and placing them in a plastic bin. Melancholy seeped over her.

She stood as his footsteps crunched toward her in the quiet of the garden.

His expression seemed downcast, but he gave a tentative smile as he neared her.

"Now, Mr. Gifford, if you are through destroying our garden, I'll take you to see the roses. We didn't destroy them."

He froze at the edge of the bed. His smile faded. "Perhaps I should help you with this first."

Tya shook her head. "I'll come back to it."

Still he stood, his gaze fixated on her.

"Are you coming? Don't just stand there like a stunned mullet." Tya turned and strode down the side of the smashed corn crop.

***

Blake stumbled after her, only catching up in time to see her disappear through a wisteria covered archway. He stepped through the arch and stopped.

The sound of water dissipated the silence. He stood on one side of a small hexagonal garden designed around two rose bushes on either side of a small pond. The garden grew lush and bright with petunias in pinks and lavenders spreading in the bed like a magical carpet. The paths and the center had been paved in grey stone. On every second side stood female statues in white. And all around, lavender wisteria draped the fence.

She stood to one side, motionless.

His knees trembled. He took a deep breath rose perfume as he stepped forward. On the surface of the pond water lilies floated and below he could see the flicker and flash of goldfish. The splashing of the fountain seemed almost musical.

He looked for the plaque and found it set in concrete at the feet of the female statue holding a water bowl on her shoulder. The words on the plaque glowed richly golden. Evidently polished by someone with love—one of the strangers whose illegal garden surrounded his memorial. Humbled, he stepped back, sank into the wooden seat placed off to one side. He buried his face in his hands and sobbed.

When he finally looked up, he was alone. Something had changed inside him; his anger had been replaced by peace. He knew he could leave his mother here with the guerilla gardeners and she would be safe. Drained by the emotional storm he had endured he staggered a little as he made his way from the oasis of peace.

The delicate light of sunset bathed the garden in pink golden glow. Tya crouched in the middle of the ruined crop tugging the cobs from the broken stalks. The other four gardeners had vanished, but he could hear water running in the distance.

She stopped rummaging through the damaged plants and looked up.

What the hell could he say? No words would justify his actions nor repair the damage.

The misery in her expression cut through him.

Should I offer to help or just jump in and start? Uncertainty held him back. They stared at each other. Blake struggled to find the right words.

He studied the wreckage he'd caused and the lone woman picking up the broken pieces. *In a fit of rage, I've demolished the back fence, a composting system, one corn crop, and two sides of the bedding border. Damn. I'm an idiot. I need to make amends if I am going to further my relationship with Tya.*

Unable to find any words to mend the angst in her posture and movements he stepped up into the bed and bent to retrieve corn cobs from the debris.

She ignored him.

They worked in strained silence for a good twenty minutes before she hesitated, and studied the ground.

He waited.

Finally, she looked across at him. "Are you satisfied we have not violated your mother's memory?" Her tone sharp with condemnation, but jagged as if she'd been crying.

Blake shook his head. "What can I say. It's beautiful. You can keep your garden—for as long as you want."

"Forever?"

A tiny ripple of amusement slipped though him. He stood, stepped toward her and placed the recovered cobs in her tub. He crouched down in front of her. The last of the sunlight bathed her in light, her hair a silver halo of tinsel on top of her head, her hands covered in dark earth.

She held her hands wide. "Well?"

It stirred again deep below the scars of the past—a warm tendril of emotion. This woman before him had guts. But that wasn't what touched his soul. Her wild beauty, her spirit, the way she seized the day and her lack of fear. Everything about her intrigued him. He knew right then he wanted to get to know this woman much better. With a slight second of hesitation he reached out and brought both her hands into his clasp. He cradled them.

She didn't pull away.

He looked into her eyes.

She stared back at him.

The air between them hummed with expectation, desire, and uncertainty.

Her bottom lip trembled, her eyes widened, and she slid the tip of her tongue over the fullness of her bottom lip.

Blake's throat tickled. He swallowed.

With the gentleness of a light summer breeze, he ran his thumbs across her soil darkened fingers. He parted her clenched hands and not caring about the soil lifted one hand and placed a slow lingering kiss in the palm. He repeated the gesture with her second hand.

The pulse in her wrist beat a frantic rhythm. She lifted her hand from his and rested it against his cheek.

Every hair in his designer stubble danced. He pressed his cheek into her palm.

With a sensuous stroke she slid her hand down his face, over his jaw and down his naked chest.

Shivers raced across his skin. His legs trembled. His crotch ached.

"Blake, I..." She leaned forward and sank to her knees. Her gaze locked with his. Her hands fell to her sides.

Blake breathed deeply. He shuffled forward a fraction and knelt.

They faced each other, in motionless silence, surrounded by the wreckage of the corn stalks.

Blake reached out and stoked her cheek before he cupped her face in both hands. He leaned toward her.

She closed the gap a tiny fraction. Her lids fluttered as she parted her lips and tilted her head.

Yearning swamped him.

The space between them crackled with passion.

He moved closer bridging the gap. His lips touched hers in a whisper soft caress. An exquisite fire seared between them.

"My God, Tya, I want you, need you," he murmured against the soft silkiness of her lips. Then he explored deeper, opening his mouth and thrusting his tongue into her, tasting her, inviting her to respond to his ardor.

She sank against him.

He embraced her, holding her mouth captive.

A soft moan escaped against his lips. He hardened his plundering discovery of her mouth.

She answered his demands.

With breathless reluctance they pulled apart.

"Be mine, Tya..."

With a shocking suddenness she pulled away from him, slumping back onto her heels. Her eyes filled with despair.

Shocked into stillness by her unexpected withdrawal, Blake stared at her. "Tya…"

She shook her head. "Don't, Blake, I can't be yours, ever."

He shook his head. "I don't understand. Don't you feel it? Tell me you feel it?"

Tears sprang up in her eyes, clouding the clear blue. She swiped them away with her hand leaving a small trail of soil across her cheek.

Blake reached out to brush it away.

She jerked back out of reach. "Don't touch me. Please don't make this harder than it already is."

A weight dropped onto his chest. "Tya, I don't understand."

She pushed to her feet. "I should never have let you kiss me, Blake."

He looked up at her. "Why, because of Stephanie and her baby. I'm not a bastard Tya she was unfaithful on our wedding day."

She shook her head. "It's only partly that but I can't, don't want to tell you the rest. It's my dishonor to bear." Her voice cracked.

The glisten of tears shone on her cheeks as she rose, turned, and fled into the vegetation.

"Tya?"

Only the whisper of the gully breeze rustled in the silence.

She had long gone by the time he shoved his way through the gate and out onto the road.

He considered following her but already sagging under the emotional aftermath of this afternoon he decided against it. They both needed some time and space to heal their shattered essences.

CHAPTER 5

With her time limited Tya hurried through the chores at the garden and headed home. Part of her sizzled with excitement, while her more practical self, dreaded the tangle she had allowed herself to get into by having dinner with Blake.

The specter of her background loomed large and threatening. Her face burned with shame every time she visualized the moment he found out. She had seen it all before and the thought of seeing that expression on Blake's face made her heartsick. *Why did I agree to have dinner? Why? I know the outcome. Stupid, stupid woman.*

Endeva grabbed Tya's arm as they turned into their street.

"Is that him—waiting for you?" Endeva whispered pulling Tya to an untidy halt.

Tya could see the metallic blue Mustang parked across the road. She shivered with anticipation and apprehension. "Probably."

"You should send him away. He's not for the likes of you and he's got that woman carrying his kid. Only buying yourself heartache."

Tya nodded. "He says she was unfaithful on the wedding day, maybe before that, but I don't know. Besides I know I'm not for the likes of him, Endeva. I'm not for the likes of any self-respecting male, but then I'm not expecting or looking for marriage or even long-term commitment."

"There you go again, putting yourself down. You gotta let go of the past and trust the future, but not by falling in love with someone so far out of your reach he might as well be the moon."

Tya smiled in the darkness and patted the older woman's shoulder. "I'm in no danger from him, but a girl deserves a little fun from time to time, even one as broken as me."

"If you say so," Endeva replied. "But know this; he's as broken as you. I can tell. You mark my words, missy, he's heart break territory."

Tya heard the disapproval in her friend's tone but chose to ignore it. She might make flippant comments about no strings sex, but it didn't appeal to her. She wasn't like her mother. She wanted love, commitment, faithfulness, but didn't expect to ever get it. Time with Blake would be a fleeting taste of what she couldn't have. She knew then why she'd agreed to have dinner with him.

"I don't plan on falling in love with him especially as some pregnant female is claiming he's the father." Disquiet slipped through her. *I don't plan on it.*

"And you can plan for that? I think not. He won't take kindly to your background either, missy. He's an attorney and his father is one of the biggest real estate and construction moguls in Australia."

Endeva's tasty little revelation hit Tya with a coward punch to the head that almost felled her physically as well as mentally. *Holy shit, my family reeks of criminals.* Nausea washed over her. *Why did she have to fall so spectacularly the only time she let her guard down in years.* Oh well, too late now, she'd promised him dinner. And that would have to be it. The end.

The empty car sat close to the curb.

She looked up and down the deserted street before turning into her garden. The instant she pushed through her gate shivers of awareness flittered over her skin. From somewhere up ahead, concealed by the gloom, and the shadows, cast by the over grown trees his scent tantalized her nostrils. She moved forward with wary steps but still jumped when he moved forward from the shadows.

"Good evening, Tya, I've been waiting to take you out to dinner."

She glanced at her fit bit. "I'm not late."

He smiled. "No, you're not. I'm just eager."

"Really. Well I won't be long then," Tya muttered.

Her mind jumped from thought to thought with desperate urgency. How she could get away with not inviting him in. A heavy blanket of embarrassment wrapped around her. The inadequacies of her home and budget loomed large in her mind but his immediate presence gave her no choice.

He followed her to the door. Her heart beat in a rapid tattoo. She fumbled for her key and again cursed the lack of a security light on the front verandah.

He stood beside her, silently waiting for her to open the door.

When she stepped through the door, he followed right behind. Tya cringed inside. She couldn't afford luxuries. Everything might be clean, but secondhand, and pretty shabby.

"Welcome to my place. Would you like a drink while you wait? I only have soft drink or juice though." She shrank some more inside—it seemed unsophisticated having no alcohol to offer. But it seemed even more demeaning to explain that she didn't have it in the house just in case she took to the drink one night and followed in the footsteps of the rest of her family and became an alcoholic.

He smiled. "Juice would be great thanks. Do you get it from the market?"

"I do. Apple is my favorite."

"My sister's too. Good stuff."

It only took a moment to produce the drink.

He smiled as he took it.

Tya flinched. *I'm burying myself in trouble here.*

"Make yourself comfortable, I won't be long."

"No rush," he replied sinking into one of her beat up old recliners and picking up one of her books on opals.

She retreated to her room, grabbed a quick shower behind a locked bathroom door then took a deep breath, and flung open both doors of her wardrobe. *What do I wear? Depends on location, but then he's only got jeans and a nice shirt on, might have a jacket in car. Oh blast, what?*

Even as she debated, she spied her black and white spotted dress, again a fifties style, that teamed with the red jacket Endeva had given her and the little red belt she had found at the market a few weeks ago. Should be fine. She peeped out the door as she spiked her hair. He seemed comfortable and engrossed in the book.

He cradled the book gently in his large hands, with a certain respect, and he turned each page by carefully lifting the top corner between a long shapely finger and thumb. As he settled back in the sagging chair, he crossed his legs tightening the denim around his thighs and creasing it over his crotch. His chest rose and fell slightly as he breathed. Several strands of his long hair had escaped his bun and dangled over his forehead. Stubble darkened his jaw.

She swallowed. Her body hummed with the desire to go and kneel between his knees and slowly undo the buttons of his shirt to expose the muscular chest behind. She shook her head. *Steady up girl or you will be playing with fire before you know it. But how I want him.*

She turned away knowing she would have to keep a tight rein on her desire tonight or she would end up with him in her bed. Having him look so at home in her dilapidated house unsettled her. Such humble surroundings were definitely not what he was used to. He would be in no doubt now she was a girl from the wrong side of the tracks—she shouldn't have to explain any more why she turned down his invitation.

She completed her preparations with a generous spray of her favorite perfume, another gift from Endeva.

He looked up from the book as she entered the room. His gaze slid over her body right to her shoes then came back up to settle on her eyes. Appreciation showed in the dark depths of his eyes and his Adam's apple jumped in his throat.

"Mmmm, very nice." He kept his gaze on her as he put the book down.

Heat scuttled up her face. "Thank you, Blake." Her knees weakened as the simmering warmth inside burst into life.

With a lithe movement he rose out of the chair and came to stand beside her. His heat radiated to her.

"Shall we go—it's such a lovely evening I thought something down by the water would nice, what do you think?"

"Lovely."

He rested his hand on her elbow.

The touch sent frissons dancing over her skin. Her knees weakened as his masculine vibes entwined themselves around her. She barely made it down the path and into the car without stumbling as her body ached with desire to be ravished. It had been a long time, but as usual her background twisted in her mind and complicated the whole issue.

As he opened the car door, he rested his hand in the small of her back.

Her skin tingled. She looked up to find him closer than she expected. The scent of his cologne swirled around them.

The intenseness of his gaze caressed her face leaving a stab of breathless desire in its wake.

She hauled in a deep breath then stopped as she realized his gaze had dropped to the soft swell of her breasts as they peeked over the neckline of her dress with the expansion of her lungs. She looked back at him.

He smiled and lifted his eyebrows a tiny fraction. He placed his hand on her elbow. "Mind your head the car is pretty low slung."

She slipped into the leather seat.

He shut the door with a small thud.

What have I got myself into he's making love to me with his eyes and I'm letting him. I want him to.

He slid into the driver's seat, pulled his belt. He looked across at her. "Comfortable?"

She nodded, unable to speak her throat tight with an emotional bubble of responsiveness.

As they drove, awareness throbbed around them in the close confines of the car. Did the man beside her feel it? She clutched her handbag tightly almost overwhelmed with the desire to touch him, to run her fingers up his arm through the light sprinkling of hairs covering the tanned skin.

His hands moved with easy familiarity on the steering wheel while the lights outside lit his rugged profile accentuating the angular planes and the strong square jaw.

Suddenly he glanced at her. "I'm glad you said yes."

Tya couldn't read his expression in the darkness. "Don't get any ideas; this is just to discuss the garden, nothing else."

He chuckled. "If you say so."

Tya squirmed inside. He knows I want him and that I'm turned on by his nearness. But then he hadn't made any secret about his desires either. Trepidation mixed with anticipation burned through her. She couldn't deny she wanted him any more than she could ignore her background.

As they walked across the car park, he placed his hand lightly on the small of her back.

She started at the contact.

He made no attempt to withdraw. Instead, he moved closer and whispered in her ear. "Such a beautiful night, made even more beautiful by the company."

"Blake, please, don't read more into my presence than there is because it will be a recipe for disaster."

"Not listening," he replied in a sing song cadence.

Tya prickled with unease. Tonight, was a mistake. With his obvious interest and her barely hidden erotic craving for his body they were already on dangerous ground. She cursed the complications, always snapping at her heels. If only she could give into her desires without questioning the rights or wrongs or the perceptions of the morning after—her own and his.

The waiter seated them by the open French doors. A full moon hung in the sky laying a trail of gold across the glassy surface of the sea. The ebb and flow of the tide gently whooshed and hissed as the waves rode up the sand blended with the soft background music. The candle in the middle of the table flickered casting faint shadows on the white cloth.

Unease whispered across her. The setting could not have been more romantic if it had been planned. It would not help the business tone she planned to set for the evening.

"Do you like crayfish, Tya?"

She smiled as a heated flush of embarrassment rush up her face and neck. "Actually, I can't say. I've never had crayfish, but I enjoy prawns."

"In that case we'll have both and some Morton Bay bugs as well. Then you can try them all. Now, what can I order for you to drink?"

"Just soft drink, thanks—lemonade."

He frowned slightly. "If you're sure? I could order a nice wine."

Tya shook her head and sighed with relief when he ordered two lemonades.

"Tell me how you got started with the garden?" Blake asked. "What made you choose my block?"

Tya laughed. "You were as mad as hell yesterday. I was so scared you'd drive right over me."

Blake smiled. "I was angry enough to be tempted, but when I saw you standing there all fired up and ready to protect your crops with your life I fell in love and just couldn't do it."

"Falling in love with me is not an option, Blake, but I'm glad you changed your mind."

He grinned. "I'm not angry anymore. You preserved the rose bushes and didn't disturb her ashes. The garden is a more than fitting memorial to my mother—she was a keen gardener."

"What happened to her, Blake?"

He shook his head. "She died a gruesome death—murdered by a drug addict."

She shuddered as her background loomed ugly and shameful. "That's awful. So sad."

"It devastated our family. For quite a few years it was just Dad and me. Potential stepmothers came and mostly at my behest, went. Then Dad met Alice and despite my horrendous behavior toward her, she refused to leave or hate me." He gave a rueful smile. "They've been together twelve years. Alice is great for my father."

"You still miss your mother?"

Blake nodded. "Not like I did at first, but I always feel her absence. I probably wouldn't have come to the block at all except it would have been her fiftieth birthday yesterday and my property manager complained about the water usage."

"Sorry about that. I know what we do is legally wrong, but we can help so many people and the land was just lying there going to waste. If you decide we have to pay for the water we'll have to stop. None of us has the money to pay and despite your assumption that we make a killing at the market we just get enough from the market to purchase expendable supplies and make a small regular donation to Endeva's charity putting defibrillators in every shop, club and pub in South Australia. You see Endeva's husband died of a heart attack so it means a lot to her."

"I can understand that and no, Tya, I'm not going to charge you for the water. You can keep the garden and use the water. It's only small change for me. Besides now I know my mother is safe I like the thought of you being there keeping her company."

"Thank you, Blake," she replied as the waiter placed the seafood platter in the middle of the table.

While they shared the food, Tya rattled on about the garden and how they covered costs but always needed things such as mulch and manure. She talked for a while about her plans to renovate her house almost as if she needed to explain to him its rundown condition.

"So how long have you lived there?"

She smiled. "Almost four years. I inherited it from my uncle when he died of cancer. I've replaced the roof and most of the plumbing. The next big job is the electrical work, but money is hard to come by when you're building your own business."

"And that is?"

Virtual PA. I only have three significant clients, but I'm working on promoting myself online and to bricks and mortar businesses, especially small business. I also make jewelry and sell at the markets."

"If you give me a couple of business cards—I'm happy to spruik for you."

"But you have no idea about the quality of my work." Her face warmed with discomfiture.

"I'm sure it will be excellent."

Tya looked down at her plate, not sure what to say. The thought of handing over her cards with her full name petrified her. Her surname identified her background without her having to say anything at all.

"Don't do a shrinking violet on me, Tya; nearly every business needs a leg up at some stage."

"Thank you, again, Blake."

He grinned. "My pleasure to help and to have your company."

"Tell me about yourself, Blake."

"I'm a lawyer and I've just got back from Hawaii. I ran away like a coward when my bride had sex with the best man just before the wedding but had to come home for my father, he had a triple bypass. He nearly died."

Tya froze. *God damn. Endeva had warned her.* She had to bring a halt to their association as soon as possible. Then again if he found out about her background he would soon disappear. A lawyer is not going to want to be associated with the likes of her. "That is terrible for you Blake. The pregnant woman at the market was she your fiancé?"

He nodded. "Sorry for dragging you into it. It's a complication I hadn't been expecting."

"Do you think it's your child?"

Blake shrugged. "I don't know Tya and I probably shouldn't be getting involved with you till I work that out, but I couldn't help myself."

"We're not getting involved Blake. This is just dinner. A business dinner."

He smiled. "I'd like to get involved Tya."

"No Blake, that's not possible."

"Because of the child?"

Tya grimaced. "Partly but Blake I'm not the right woman for you. Can we just leave it at that."

He shrugged and took some more seafood from the platter. "I've sold my law practice recently. I had enough dealing with the low lifes, the scum and the downright evil. Besides I have to take over my father's company at least for now. I'm not sure what I'm going to do long term. I like having balance in my life, surfing, and working with a couple of charities. Later I might investigate politics, but I'm not sure if I can follow any particular party. It might have to be as an independent."

Again, the shadow of doom washed over her. Politics. "That's a cutthroat game isn't it?

He nodded. "Lots of back stabbing and reputation blackening, but it means one can actually do something to make the world a better place."

Tya grimaced. "I'll stick to gardening and feeding the masses as my contribution to bettering the world."

Blake grinned back.

At Blake's revelations a wave of sickness and anxiety washed over Tya. The last thing she would want is her background dug up and exposed to the world. But despite the inevitable short life of her time with Blake she wasn't quite ready to banish him.

They decided not to have dessert but get an ice-cream down the road.

He pulled on his jacket before they left the restaurant and when Tya shivered a little as they stepped outside into the cool sea breeze, he helped her with hers.

As they walked slowly down the esplanade, the gentle swish of the sea on the sandy shore in the background Blake drifted closer to her side.

His body heat radiated against her skin. His masculine aura enveloped her as it teased her senses and called to her soul.

When his fingers curled around hers, she flinched, but didn't pull away.

He veered even closer until they were walking shoulder to shoulder. Every step he took brought him into closer contact until he leaned lightly against her. He steered her along the jetty, their footsteps echoing on the aged boards.

The wooden structure amplified the rhythmic swish of the sea below them.

They ambled slowly, the silver moonlight streaming across the bay leaving a soft glow rippling over the ocean.

The lights were low in places and Blake stopped in one of the dim spots and turned to face her. He continued to hold one of her hands and with his free hand he softly stroked her cheek.

She stood as if captured in a spotlight, staring up at him, soaking up the sizzling touch of his skin against hers. Her heart beat erratically, anticipation flashed through her, yet she made no move to prevent him from completing his intention.

He stepped closer.

Her breasts brushed against his shirt as she breathed the salty tang of the air with shallow irregular huffs.

With his free hand he cupped her jaw thoughtfully outlining the curve of the bone with his thumb. He stared unblinkingly into her eyes, the expression in his almost daring her to pull away.

She didn't want to pull away even though alarm bells rattled in her head. She licked lips suddenly dry with expectancy, swallowed, and parted her lips slightly offering a blatant invitation.

He lowered his head, blocking out the moonlight.

She lowered her eyelids as his lips touched hers, a teasing feather light touch for the briefest moments before it was gone. As she registered his withdrawal, his mouth claimed hers, hard, a commanding jousting of sensitive flesh against sensitive flesh. His demanding, hers responding—giving, tasting, teasing the mellow fire within each to the point of ignition—a tumultuous explosion that rocked both of them to the core.

Tya pulled away gasping, every inch of her body trembling.

Blake held her shoulders in a desperate grip as he struggled with his own control.

His hands trembled even as they clutched the softness of her upper arms.

Her cool thoughts of what this encounter should be, scattered in a shower of blistering stars of desire. A scorching trail of lust blazed through her body, leaving her stunned and static in his hands.

When she made no attempt to move away, he released her shoulders and cupped her face with both his hands, tipped her head back, cradled it in one hand, lowered his head and covered her mouth with his.

She melted inside, the throbbing between her legs pulsating upwards; in total surrender she collapsed against him, immediately feeling the hardness of his erection. Suddenly shy she went to pull away.

One of his hands grasped her buttocks, lifted her and pressed her tighter against his crotch. His chest heaved as he plundered her mouth, delving deep inside, entwining her tongue with his.

Almost of their own volition her arms wrapped around his waist and completed their circle of closeness until only their clothes stopped his cock from burrowing into her.

The world spun in a sparkling spiral of stars, as a lack of oxygen blanketed her brain.

Blake let out a muffled groan and released her mouth with a lingering caress. He heaved in some air then crushed her against his chest. "My God, Tya, I've waited so long for you," he spluttered on the outward breath. "So, God damn long."

She stood motionless in his embrace, the cold dread of her own reality pressing between them, dampening the roaring embers of desire.

The weight of his chin rested on the top of her head. "Now I've found you, I'm never letting you go," he mumbled in her hair.

Tya wriggled against his restraint. She couldn't let the delusion continue unabated. She had to make it clear—they had no future.

"Blake, stop. There can be no us—ever. I'm no good for you."

He let her slip from his embrace. "Don't say that, Tya. I know you feel it. Tell me you feel it?"

She stepped back, breaking the contact with him and nodded. "Yes, I feel it, but feelings lie—here one minute, gone the next. They won't stand up to reality. You and me, we live in different worlds, mine is ugly, yours is all roses and champagne."

"No, Tya, nothing to do with you could ever be ugly."

She grimaced. "You don't know it all. Please let it be, we've had a lovely night, but that is all there can be."

He shook his head.

"I'm sorry, Blake. Please take me home."

He took her hand, and she didn't pull away, needing his touch to help hold her heart and soul together until she could be alone to cry the demise of her momentary fairytale.

Halfway into the drive Blake cleared his throat and glanced at her before he looked back at the road. "Tya, if it is the fact you only have a small income stopping you getting involved with me I can assure you it doesn't matter. My father grew up poor."

"But you didn't"

"No, but my father has never let me forget our roots."

"Exactly, one should never forget one's roots. Please let it be."

"Tya, please, tell me. I've fallen in love with you. Nothing you can tell me will change that."

Tears stung her eyes. She so wanted to pour it all out but couldn't bear to see the revulsion or disgust in his eyes. Better she kept her secrets and remembered his grey eyes soft with desire for her.

"I can't tell you because I don't want to see the repugnance in your eyes. It's better we part now, as strangers. You'll be glad one day."

"No, I won't."

A tense silence filled the car for the remainder of the journey.

She struggled to get out of the car.

Blake sat staring through the windscreen. He hadn't questioned her anymore after he bluntly refuted her statement.

As she went to close the door he turned to her. "You won't re-consider, Tya?"

She shook her head. "I can't. Goodbye, Blake." She shut the door with a thud.

In a rumble of horsepower and waft of exhaust fumes Blake roared down her street, around the corner and out of sight.

With barely enough strength in her legs to carry her to the front door, Tya staggered down the path, fumbled to open the door and almost fell inside. She made it two steps to the old recliner and collapsed into its sagging seat. Tears flooded down her cheeks and her throat twisted with choking sobs. Tonight, had been a big mistake. Gutted by the denial of her very nature, the passion, the craving for love and the downright lusty need she felt stripped of her dignity and pride. In that moment she hated her mother with savage defiant rage.

She lay for a long time staring at the ceiling, cursing the dilemma she found herself in. No matter how much she wanted Blake she couldn't let herself indulge because too much hurt lurked around the corner. She closed her eyes and the dreams came. Dreams of wild loving with

Blake. Her mother peeping in at the window laughing and making accusations—you're a whore just like me. Then Blake appeared sitting on the bench thudding his gavel and declaring her guilty.

CHAPTER 6

With the day promising to break records in the temperature stakes Tya climbed out of bed before the sky lightened with dawn. The early start didn't bother her because she hadn't been sleeping anyway, just tossing and turning, her head full of jumbled thoughts and her heart cringing with anguish. *A lawyer, politics and a baby on the way. God damn it, it couldn't be any worse.*

Convinced it would come back to haunt her, and him, she fought the idea in her head but had already lost the battle in her body.

She moved through the green forest almost silently, hitching shade cloth to stakes, soaking the rich ground with cool water and picking all the fruit that showed any signs of ripening. With the heat it would be past its best by tonight—cooked even.

At seven she paused for a coffee settled in a chair for a moment's peaceful meditation.

A loud horn blast from the back of the property rattled along her nerves and completely shattered her quiet contemplation. She splashed the dregs of her coffee on the ground and jumped out of the chair. With frown crinkling her brow Tya glanced over her shoulder.

A couple of burly blokes stood in the jagged opening left by the bulldozer.

"Where do you want the mulch and fertilizer, love? I figured here at the back would be best."

"What fertilizer and mulch? I didn't order anything."

"No, but I did." Blake popped up beside the two men. "It's a peace offering after my lunacy the other day."

Every nerve ending tingled, confusion rattled her composure and strangled her words. A sharp awareness of this man whispered over her skin. "Stop, Blake," she croaked. "You don't have to do this."

He came to stand in front of her.

The scent of his spicy cologne tantalized her nostrils.

He reached out and softly ran his hand down her cheek.

Her skin shivered with knowing and needing.

"Yes, I do Tya. I need to apologize, sincerely. What I did was unreasonable, unforgivable. I won't make excuses, but I will make amends. Besides you will not get rid of me that easily despite your self-deprecation."

Tya stared up at him, her breathing short, puffy and erratic. "You should have taken notice."

His chest also rose and fell with irregular jerks. He stared down at her.

She drowned in the grey depths of his eyes. Her body purred with awareness. The heady mixture of desire swirled around them.

He moved closer.

She leaned towards him. Inner alarm bells shuddered through her. He intended to kiss her. That was not a good idea. Not now. Not ever.

He placed one hand either side of her face.

She tensed but couldn't bring herself to back away.

He loomed in.

His breath warm and minty against her skin. The soft hiss of his breathing as inconsistent as hers. Invisible sparks sizzled between them as she leaned toward him. No matter her protest and the danger of the inevitable crash and burn she made no attempt to stop it. She wanted him.

She kept her eyes open until the last minute as his head blocked out the sun and his mouth touched hers. Desire burst inside her. Liquid warmth gathered in her pussy as she pressed against the hard rod of his erection. A desperate need surged through her. She craved his loving. It had been a long time since she had shared her body with a man.

As his mouth broke contact, he whispered against her cheek. "I can bring anything I like, it's my land" He lifted her face up to him. "You do need the stuff, I assume?"

Tya nodded.

Blake grinned as he let his hands slide away. "Good." With a brisk movement he tugged his tee over his head to reveal a sculptured chest and muscular arms. "By the way the new rotary hoe will arrive tomorrow."

Tya almost swooned. She shoved her hands into her pockets to prevent herself from reaching out and touching the golden skin.

Immediately he bent over the bags and moved them into the shed.

Tya watched, fascinated by supple play of hard muscle under smooth tanned skin.

A sheen of perspiration soon appeared on his naked torso accentuating the play of light and shadow on the undulating angles of his body.

Tiny pinpricks of arousal scattered teasingly along her pussy leaving a sweet ache of need in its trail. She clenched her hands deep in her pockets in a desperate effort to thwart her need to reach out and touch him—to stoke and caress the hard satin of his skin.

"What's this then?" Endeva asked from right behind her.

Tya jumped as she rudely thudded back to the real world. "A gift from Blake, mulch and fertilizer."

"What's the trade off?"

Tya shrugged. "There is none."

Endeva placed her hand firmly on Tya's shoulder. "You better watch yourself, young lady. He's trouble, that one. Man, like him doesn't give like that for nothing."

"Oh Endeva, he's just wanted to make amends for his little temper tantrum."

"Hmmmp. You better be careful, girl. That's all, just be careful."

Frustration and anger surged through her at her friend for shattering her lovely daydreams. Already a cold lump of dread weighed her down. Endeva spoke the truth.

Tya nodded, already feeling the inevitable outcome of their interaction stalking her. She wanted him. Despite all her misgivings and the possible repercussions of getting involved she knew she was going to do it regardless. It would be a little something for her.

It took the three men and some minimum assistance from Tya and Endeva less than half an hour to unload the truckload of supplies into the shed and by the beds already marked out for new crops. The temperature had already soared into the mid-thirties.

As Blake prowled towards her every inch of his skin sheened with perspiration, his shorts hung low on his hips revealing just a few dark springy hairs above the waist band.

He gulped some iced water. "I'm off. I have a site inspection to supervise before the heat. Tya, do you need a lift home?"

She shook her head. "Thanks, but I still have a bit of watering to do."

"Okay, see you tonight to spread the stuff."

"But you don't have to..."

He stepped closer to her and ran his finger down her cheek. "I know, but I want too, and it brings me closer to you."

He snatched up his shirt, pulled it on as he disappeared through the rows of tomatoes.

Tya stood for a long time staring after him. His charisma tugged at her. Yearning for love entangled her in an inescapable web of lust, love and unadulterated chemistry of two reluctant soul mates.

The inevitable loomed over her, mocking her, daring her to fight its primeval call. God damn it, I want him—all of him, in her life, in her bed and in her body. She sighed, deep and heavy. Why the hell can't I stay away when I know it's dangerous and complicated?

No answer to her dilemma presented itself as she moved sluggishly through the rows flooding the soil in the hope it would remain damp until tonight. The weather girl had promised a cool change for tomorrow.

The sun already blasted the city with stinging rays as she slipped inside her front door. She put on the new split system she'd invested in for the office, had a cool shower and settled down to work. It took a couple of coffees and some fiddling before she re-captured her focus and set about balancing Deemonde Impacts' invoices, payments and incomings. By the time she had reconciled everything, even the cooler struggled to combat the scorching heat.

She picked up a book and settled on the lounge to read and wait out the stifling temperature, but she struggled to concentrate on her book with thoughts of Blake intruding uninvited. She pondered the jilted bride, Stephanie and the current state of her relationship with Blake. And their unborn child. Well maybe it was his.

Not that it should be her concern if Blake still had feelings for his jilted bride. But even knowing they had no future she didn't want to be used as a distraction until he got his real relationship back on track. He must have once had strong feelings for her since he planned to marry her. He had made it clear why he had jilted her. Briefly Tya pondered future entanglements and possibilities before casting the intrusive thoughts aside.

Just as he'd promised Blake turned up barely half an hour after Tya arrived dressed for the task at hand in blue tradies' work shorts, a singlet tee and work boots. A couple of the new shovels dangled from his hand.

Blake, Dave and Jordan set about shoveling and spreading the compost.

As she watched the three men work side by side her breath caught in her throat. She tried to breathe softly but her heart did a little dance in her chest. Tingling vibes ran along her nerve endings and pooled between her legs.

"Hey, put your tongue back in, missy, it ain't yours."

Tya flapped her hand at Endeva and continued to perve and drool. "I can't help it."

Blake suddenly paused, lifted his head and looked directly at her. He lifted one hand and brushed the stray strands of hair from his face. Tya shivered under the intensity of his brooding stare. Then he smiled, full lips curving up ever so slightly.

Heat seared through her.

His look said it all. He must have sensed her staring at him, drinking in his untamed masculinity.

Tya vaguely heard her friend rattling on about consequences and heart break through the haze of awareness that held her paralyzed.

"Shhh, Endeva, I..." Tya's voice cracked and faded as her gaze locked with his.

Amusement contorted into pure unadulterated desire as his smile widened. His blazing gaze captured and held her as he walked slowly toward the shed. He groped blindly for a bottle of water in the cooler. In one smooth movement he grabbed one, opened the lid and drank slowly. A small dribble dropped onto his chest and slid down in a lazy slide.

Tya watched it transverse the undulating muscles. The desire to step up to him and lick it from his skin whipped over her.

He looked directly at her his expression full of the fiery promise to ravish her.

The hair danced on her skin. Warmth pooled in her nether regions.

She stirred restlessly.

Blake smiled, just a small smile that tweaked up one side of his mouth. He knew she had received his message loud and clear.

Desire scorched through her. She swallowed, licked her lips with the tip of her tongue. In an attempt to break free, she lowered her gaze, only to find herself staring directly at his crotch. Shudders tore through her as she ripped her gaze away and brought it back to his face.

His expression blazed unrequited desire as he tipped a little of the iced water over his shoulders and chest leisurely spreading the water with a big hand. He left a muddy trail on his skin that only served to accentuate the tightly pumped muscles. He put the bottle of water back in the cooler and raised his eyebrows just a little as he casually wiped his muddy hands across the front of his shorts. Tya watched the movement of his hands, shivered and gasped in a tight breath of air, choked on it, coughed and let the shudders of arousal rumbled through her. Tya licked her lips again.

"Come on, Blake, bring some more bags or we won't be done by dark."

Without hesitation, Blake picked up a bag of cow manure.

Tya gasped at the swiftness he transitioned from seducing her to gardener.

His muscles flexed and tightened as he scooped up a second bag and strode with long smooth strides for the garden bed. "On my way, fellas."

His voice, husky and warm flowed like golden honey over her tingling nerve endings – soothing, enticing and very, very, engaging.

Tya stared after him her body humming anew at his tightly encased backside. Another quiver vibrated through her and pooled in her pussy. She tightened her muscles instinctively against the sensation and barely muffled a yearning moan that rose unexpectedly.

"I have never seen such a spectacle in all my life, Tya Morley. You should be ashamed of yourself. You just about crawled into his pants," Endeva spluttered the moment they were out of earshot.

Tya sagged into her chair, shaking her head. "I couldn't help it – it was like he had me under a spell. Oh my God, I couldn't take my eyes off him."

"Yes, well. That was obvious for all to see, panting, jiggling and sighing. What's got into you?"

Fresh heat rushed up Tya face. She didn't know what to say so she just shook her head.

"You've always told me you have no intention of getting involved—that you aren't made for a relationship."

"I'm not made for a relationship—nothing has changed. But I never said I couldn't appreciate a hunk when one walks into my life and literally seduces me with his eyes."

"Yes, well you had better mind yourself, young lady. You've already had dinner with him. What's next? He's a sexy bugga, I'll grant you that, young Tya, but best you leave well alone."

"I know, Endeva, with my tortured background I'm not fit for someone like that—in fact any one at all."

"Nah, that's bullshit, Tya. Just cos your genes are shit don't mean you can't rise above it. But maybe not enough for one like him and then you'll get broken."

Tya got up and packed away the unused fertilizer. "Thanks for the vote of confidence, but I know the odds, and I'm not prepared to take the risk and muck up someone else's life like my parents did."

"You judge yourself very harshly, Tya. I know you and I don't..."

"No. Endeva, don't even go there. I'm not listening to your soothing sentiments. I know me, and I've made my decision."

Endeva spluttered into silence.

Self-reproach tugged at Tya. Poor Endeva. Endeva's heart was pure gold, but she looked at life through rose-colored glasses and would protect Tya to her last breath. Despite her defiant reply Tya knew she couldn't afford to be lulled into a false sense of security about her future.

With the corn planted and the mulch spread on the second bed Tya paused to study their progress. "All right enough for today we'll finish the rest tomorrow. "Time to go home and cool off."

"Nah, let's cool off right here," Jordon shouted and turned the hose on full and squirted Dave."

"You little whipper snapper you don't get away with that." Dave grabbed up the second hose and advanced on Jordon. Water sprayed everyone.

Endeva backed away shaking the water from her hair. "Cut it out, *children.*"

Tya glanced at her, kicked off her shoes and charged Jordon. She wrestled the hose from his hands and turned it on Blake. He brushed the water from his face and grinned.

"Now you're in trouble," he growled as he advanced.

Dave turned the hose on Tya, drenching her. She reveled in the cool water on her heated skin. She squirted Dave back but he already fought with Jordon grappling for possession of the hose. Tya turned back to Blake.

He leaned in close and reached for her hose. They tussled for it their bodies getting closer and closer.

"Wet em, Jordon."

The full blast of the water showered them. The hose slipped from her hands. Blake took command of it directing the stream straight at her torso. He breathed hard, and fast, as he advanced toward her. His eyes smoky with desire.

Jordon stalked forward. "I'll protect you, Tya."

He blasted Blake. Blake swiveled the stream of water onto his new foe just for a moment then back to Tya.

Jordon advanced. Suddenly his water spray vanished. "What the heck. Where's me water?"

"It's off, young man. Such a waste and look at the mess." Endeva stood by the tap her hands on her hips.

Blake and Tya stopped and surveyed the damage. The work area right around the shed had tuned into a sea of mud.

Tya combed back her dripping hair. "Oops. Sorry, Blake, there goes your water bill."

He grinned. "It was worth it. Everyone's nice and cool, and very wet."

Tya suddenly realized her thin white singlet top had become almost transparent when wet and in a flush of self-consciousness wished she'd worn a bra. "Well then it's time to go home."

Blake watched her. She sensed his animal interest and with Endeva's warning fresh in her mind she determined she would not get drawn into Blake's lusty aura.

"Thanks, Blake, for your help. I'll see you around okay."

"But I thought I could drive you home."

Tya shook her head. "Thanks, but I'm all wet. It's best if I walk with Endeva." Her need curled and writhed in her gut, a wave of chill throbbed in her pussy. She wanted this man, but it could never be. She had to hold him at arm's length. She didn't trust him or herself.

He shrugged and headed for the back alley where he'd parked his car. "Night all."

As they walked up the road she heard the rumble of the Mustang's powerful engine echoing up the back lane. Despite the success of her off put disappointment weighed heavy against her heart. She wanted him, so badly. Deep down she had wanted him to protest her rejection of him. It wounded her ego that he had been put off so easily.

She stood at her gate as Endeva walked the three houses to her own gate then they both turned in at the same time. Almost immediately Tya sensed a presence ahead. She paused and stared through the darkness. She couldn't see her companion, but she could smell the spicy scent of cologne. *Blake.* She glanced behind her, but the street was empty. *Damn he intended to take her by surprise.*

She climbed the steps.

He stepped out of the shadows.

"Why are you here, Blake?"

"Why? Because I want to enjoy your company and wanted to see more of you, all wet."

She fumbled in her bag for the keys as she watched him coming slowly closer. "Well you shouldn't," she said self-consciously pulling her partially dry tee away from her breasts."

"Shouldn't what?"

Her hand closed over the keys and she pulled them from her bag as she turned to face him. "You shouldn't enjoy my company or ask me out to dinner. You should put your efforts into a girl from your world, not one like me."

He took one exaggerated step to bring him to her side. He reached out and with the slightest touch stroked her nipple through the wet material. Tya gasped.

"Tell me to stop, Tya, and I will."

The words wouldn't form.

He stroked back across her nipple. It stood erect. "I don't want a woman from my world, Tya. I want you."

She stared up at him mesmerized, trembling with desire from his briefest touch. "You shouldn't want me, Blake."

He stroked across her nipple again.

She shivered. The keys jingled in her hand.

"But I want you so much." He stepped right up to her and lowered his head to claim her mouth.

She trembled. The keys jingled to the floor.

Breathless, they parted.

"Open the door, Tya."

Disorientated by the darkness and his closeness she lost her balance tipping forward, the verandah rushed up to meet her.

He grabbed her waist in the tight grip not only holding her upright but pulling her against him.

Chemistry ignited into a blazing inferno where their bodies touched.

Tya gasped as the molten fire of arousal raced through her veins. She looked up at him.

Seconds later he claimed her mouth with his. A hard, dominant, demanding exploration of her mouth.

She reached up to be closer, blatantly responding with demands of her own.

He encircled her in a commanding, almost desperate embrace and Tya pressed against his hardness letting her soft flesh mold to his.

As the heat of his erection branded her abdomen, Tya abandoned any thoughts of resisting. She may keep her emotions in cold storage, but her body's natural instinct for sexual contactrampaged out of control. She wanted this man, and she would have this man—at least for a moment or two.

His big hands cupped her buttocks and lifted her right off the ground as his mouth continued its ruthless exploration of hers. He stepped backwards.

"Open the door, Tya," he gasped against her lips.

She fumbled with shaking fingers trying to insert the key in the locks.

He pulled her closer rubbing his crotch against hers now exposed by her spread-eagled legs curling around his hips. "For God's sake woman hurry up, or I'll be taking you right here on the doorstep.

Shudders raced through her, and the muscles surrounding her pussy jerked and tingled in anticipation of his taking her body.

The lock clicked and they almost rolled inside.

Blake kicked the door shut and they staggered against the wall with Tya's back pressed against the hall table.

Taking advantage of the support Tya reached up and ripped his shirt open revealing a hard muscular chest still damp from the drenching.

He released her mouth just long enough to gasp in air and haul his shirt over his shoulders and let it drop to the floor. Then he plastered kisses on her mouth, her cheeks and nose before returning to possess her mouth again. Then he lifted her and they staggered a few steps closer to the bedroom pausing in the doorway to rebalance and allow Blake to lift her tee over her head. As they bumbled around the door jamb Blake lowered his head and sucked on one of her nipples. The deep pink flesh hardened against his tongue and the caress of his mouth sent fiery arrows of sensation spearing though her breasts.

Tya gasped at the intensity and tightened the grip of her legs around his waist pressing the soft mound sheltering her aching pussy against the mound of his erection.

He moaned as he took control of her mouth again as they staggered along the wall. He stood her down.

She immediately grappled with his belt and fly her hands shaking with anticipation and need to expose his cock and touch the hard, hot flesh.

His hands covered hers as he hastened the loosening of his pants.

They dropped to the floor.

Tya immediately dragged his trunks down. The hard rod of his flesh literally jumped towards her the shine of pre cum in the eye. She enclosed his flesh in one hand and cupped his balls with her other.

"Oh my God, Tya touch me, squeeze me." He groaned against her neck.

Tya gently applied pressure to his balls, rolling them around between her fingers as her other hand stroked leisurely up and down the rigid shaft.

Even as she concentrated on his cock, he fiddled with her shorts button. It snapped open and Blake scooped them over her buttocks and pushed impatiently until they slid together with her panties to the floor. He pressed her against the wall, sliding one hand between her legs. He parted them slightly.

Tya almost collapsed at the exquisite sensations spreading from her clit right through her pussy and down her legs. Her bones softened and she struggled to stay up right she let go of his cock and curled her arms around his shoulders.

Blake held her pinioned against the wall easing her slightly upwards as he probed between her legs with his cock.

Her body coiled in anticipation of penetration; her nerves set to explode the moment he entered.

He eased his hard flesh into her hot moist softness.

Tya stifled a scream as a bubble of fiery desire built inside her. Tremors exploded through her as his cock sank deeply into her quivering flesh. The bubble burst and splattered sensation everywhere. The room span, the light flickered, faded and brightened again. She clenched her muscles tightly around his cock as it thrust hard and deep, but she could not hold the tension as wave after wave of exquisite sensation again crashed inside her, sucking her bones of their strength and sweeping away the solidness of her flesh. She cried out each time he thrust into her, carried away by the swirling ecstasy that held her in its grip.

Sweat beaded between them as Blake thrust deep, groaned and pressed her hard against the wall as he leaned onto her in a semi stupor, the breath whistling in and out of his chest.

Then they were sagging, slipping in exhausted weakness to the floor.

Blake lay on his back one arm encircling Tya. He stared at the ceiling, his chest rising and falling, and a glistening sheen of perspiration accentuating every angle of muscle.

Tya curled against his side, but kept her eyes shut unsure how to face her lover in the aftermath of such explosive passion. Their union had been fast and ruthless, but mind-blowing, satisfying in a way she had never been satisfied. She waited in silence reluctant to look into his eyes in case he hadn't felt the same way, but afraid at the same time if he had felt the same things. Then it would be so much more complicated for her.

Satiation held them still and somewhat shy.

In the distance Tya could hear the uneven hum of the traffic up the highway and in the distance a dog barked. Another answered, closer to home. She didn't know what to do next. There had been no hesitation by either of them, but now it was over uncertainty hovered between them.

"Tya?"

"Yes."

"Should I apologize for being in such a rush? I meant to woo you subtlety, gently…"

She laid a hand on his chest. "Stop. I wanted it as much as you, as desperately as you, since the first time in the market."

He chuckled.

Tya felt the vibrations in his chest.

He eased himself onto his side. His fingers pressed on her cheek as he brought her around to face him. His smoky grey eyes were soft and his mouth curved into a smile that radiated tenderness and satiation. He traced the lines of her face with his finger. "So if I suggest we adjourn to bed and do it properly you won't object?"

Tya smiled. "No, Blake, I won't object. "

He lifted himself up on his elbow and looked down at her. With gentle fingers he stroked her cheek. "I never thought I would ever be in this position again."

"What position?"

"Falling in love with a beautiful woman."

"Blake, please don't say that. You can't fall in love with me. I'm not very loveable, it's too risky."

"But you are loveable, Tya. Very loveable."

"And Stephanie and her baby?"

Blake shook his head. "I no longer love her there will never be anything between me and Stephanie. Ever."

"Please be sure, Blake. Don't use me to make her jealous. I couldn't bear that."

He shook his head. "I won't, Tya. I'm not."

"What about the baby?"

Blake sighed deeply. "I'm not sure it's my child."

Tya pushed up on her elbow and looked down into his eyes. "But weren't you engaged, getting married? Surely, it's yours."

"Yes, and it could be my child, but I caught her with my best man an hour before the ceremony so there is doubt. They were having a right old time. That's why I left her standing at the church door. I was gutted. Now you have all the sordid gossip shall we continue this in your bed?"

Quite a while later Blake stirred. "How about we go somewhere to eat. I'm starving. You go have a shower and I'll get my spare clothes from the car."

"You have spares in the car."

"Always do. Used to go surfing, shower and change on the beach then straight to the office."

She giggled. "We could shower together, make up for the wasted water this afternoon."

He leaned down and brushed his mouth across hers. "If I come into the shower with you right now we might never get out and I'm starving."

She planted a light kiss on his mouth. "I'm hungry too so go get your clothes. I'll be quick."

He grinned and rolled out of the bed. He peered around in the gloom. "Where are my shorts?"

As he wandered naked out into the passage Tya climbed out of bed and headed for the shower.

The night was still and balmy. The sky was sprinkled with stars. The restaurant bustled with people brought out by the cooler night air.

Blake opened her door and immediately wrapped his arm around her waist. Tya snuggled into him determined to get the most out of this liaison as she could before it had to end.

They found a table and Blake ordered wine but Tya shook her head when he offered to pour it.

"Sorry, Tya, I should have remembered from the other night. You don't like wine?"

Tya shook her head. "I don't drink alcohol at all, Blake."

He frowned. "Are you a recovering alcoholic?"

Tya flinched. "No. But most of my family have addictive personalities and it frightens me that I might get addicted."

"Oh. Fair enough." He signaled the waiter. "Can we have two soft drinks please?"

Again, Tya cringed. "You don't have to abstain, Blake, just because I do."

He grinned. "I know." He reached out and curled his hand around hers squeezing it gently. "Now what do you want to eat. I can recommend the chicken and pumpkin risotto or they do a delicious steak."

Tya glanced down the menu and settled on the risotto. Blake ordered.

"So why are you so hard on yourself, Tya?"

She shook her head. "I need to keep control. It's not a strong point in my family."

Blake grinned cheekily. "Well, I didn't see much control in your response to my lovemaking."

The heat climbed up her face. She didn't know whether to be complimented or insulted.

Blake lifted her hand to his lips. "Don't be embarrassed, Tya, my love. Your response told me I was doing the right thing."

Tya giggled. "Yes, you did that."

"Blake Gifford, just the man I needed to see." The voice boomed over them as their space was crowded by an extremely tall man with long brown dreadlocks.

Blake frowned with displeasure as he looked up at their unexpected visitor.

"Connor, you're intruding."

"I won't keep you long, I just need a word."

"It's so important it can't wait until tomorrow or a phone call would have it covered."

"Nah, this is personal. Stephanie told me you know."

"Yes, I saw you going hammer and tongs, her wedding dress hitched up. Made me sick to the stomach. So, anything personal between us, mate, was decimated right then and there."

"Yeah, I thought as much, but what's this demand for DNA tests."

"I want to be sure the kid she's having is mine."

"Well, if you aren't the father then I suppose I am. I can't afford the cost of tests or maintenance for that matter."

Blake's face darkened; his mouth was drawn into a thin line. "This is not the time, or place, for this discussion, Connor."

"Nah, I suppose not. Your date is looking a bit distressed."

Blake looked at Tya, then back up to Connor. "Did Steph put you up to this?"

Connor shook his head. "Stephanie is furious you want the tests in the first place. She doesn't like being caught out."

Blake nodded. "I'll pay for the tests, Connor. Make an appointment at the Norton Clinic on Main North Road once the baby arrives. I'm not afraid to take responsibility if this baby is mine."

Connor looked at Tya. "Probably not what you date wants to hear."

"Probably not, but if he is mine, I need to do the right thing."

"What about Stephanie. She still has the hots for you."

"Yes, I know, but that has nothing to do with the child's parentage."

"So, would you take her back?"

Blake hesitated. "None of your business, Connor."

"It is if you going to be stepfather to my kid."

"God damn it, Connor, bugger off."

Connor turned and walked away without a backward look.

Blake straightened in his seat and glared at his risotto.

Tya reached out and placed her hand on his. "Would you go back to her for the sake of your son?"

Blake looked across at her. Half his face was in shadow but the soft glow of the streetlight lit the other half. Grim tautness pulled to at the corner of his mouth. "No, Tya. No, you're the only woman I want, but I must take responsibility if it is my child."

"And if you can't have me would that change your decision?"

He glowered. "No, never, but I will have you."

"You're not listening to me, Blake. We have no future. I am not the woman for you."

"Why?"

"Because I'm unsuitable."

He clutched her hand. "Don't say that."

"Please take me home, Blake. I've lost my appetite."

Blake gave her a wan smile. "Sorry, Tya."

It was a quiet drive home. Each of them consumed with their own thoughts. Tya felt betrayed but knew she wasn't really. Her life was complicated enough as it was. She could not become involved with Blake in the hope of a future. That would only bring heartache, humiliation and suffering. She had already let it go too far. Not that she regretted making love.

As Blake pulled up in front of her house Tya unclipped her seatbelt. "If the child proves to be yours you might feel differently about everything, Blake, and it's better this way for I'm not for you anyway. She opened the door. "Go home, Blake."

"Tya, please. It doesn't have to be like this."

Tya climbed out of the low-slung car. "Go sort yourself out, Blake. Please don't come back."

"You can't just walk away from what we have. You can't ignore tonight. We're meant to be together."

Tya grimaced. "Yes, I can, Blake. I don't need the complications nor do you."

She strode across the road afraid to look back, afraid she would give in and invite him in to her bed and her heart. It would do no good to let him see her tears. Her heart throbbed with each beat. How had she been so gullible after all she said about not getting involved? She had let her guard down for a moment and look what happened. *Stupid. Careless.*

He would be better off with Stephanie anyway. Sobs crowded against her diaphragm and she struggled to breathe as she slipped through her front door. The tears fell as her barely held control disintegrated. She stayed there leaning on the door, with tears streaming down her cheeks until she heard the grumble of the sports car disappear down the street.

Just because it was for the best didn't stop it hurting her. She made the bed with fresh sheets and lit a couple of scented candles to eliminate the ambiance of their sexual encounter. She lay on the top of the blankets for a long time remembering the touch of his hands and the feel of his cock being buried in her pussy. A warm waft of sexual desire flowed through her and she wondered if she should masturbate, but even as her hands caressed between her legs her eyelids drooped and with a slight sigh she drifted into sleep.

She stirred, rolled over then stretched. Satisfied contentment flowing through her body bringing a smile to her lips but as memories of their encounter and its painful end rushed back her smile faded.

Rain drops splattered on her window and pattered in a steady rhythm on her tin roof. Tya cuddled down into the quilt as waves of anguish and regret washed over her. She hiccupped the threatening sobs back into her chest and buried her face into the pillow trying to find the strength to face the day. The day after love slipped from her fingers and was cast out of her heart.

Glad she didn't have to go to the garden she prepared for the day reluctance dragging at her every move. At least the garden would love this shower of rain. It didn't seem to matter how much you watered it never did the plants the good a shower of rain did. It also saved her time this morning because she had an early appointment with the graphic designer and printer to organize a couple of large pull up banners for one of her clients.

The clock in the station had just struck seven when she caught the train. It was crowded with peak hour commuters, but she managed to find one last seat. She slipped into it and stared out the window at the passing scenery. But all she could see through the rain smeared window was a reflection of Blake's face, his eyes filled with pleasure and lust as he thrust into her. She squirmed a little on her seat as the warmth pooled in her pussy. *Damn him to hell. I never meant to get this close or this needy.* A lump of bitterness thudded deep inside. *You idiot, Tya Morley stop mooning after a man you can't have.* The reasons were clear in her mind and really Stephanie was the least of the obstacles to her loving Blake.

He was a lawyer of all things and her family was full of crime. She wouldn't be surprised if one of them had been defended by Blake. The heat of shame flushed up through her cheeks at how he hated such people and the pain of his mother's death. How had she been so stupid?

It continued to rain as she walked out of the station and across North Terrace. It wasn't particularly cold, more hot and humid, the huge drops of rain falling straight down steaming as it hit the hot pavements.

Perspiration beaded on her skin as she made her way up to the first tram stop. It was a short ride to Victoria Square and a longer walk along Grote Street. She found the graphic designer's office at the top of a narrow staircase. She had a long and frustrating meeting with the designer and came away dissatisfied with his suggestions and nothing confirmed.

She hurried along the street and slipped into the central market looking for an early lunch. It was crowded inside with shoppers seeking refuge from the rain and the heat. She found a seat in the food court and ordered a seafood salad. It was fresh and tasty.

She studied the shoppers as she ate. A familiar face arrested her gaze. Blake. She was about to call out when Stephine emerged from behind him. She slumped in her chair watching them.

Tya sat frozen, appalled at being witness to Blake's obvious rendezvous with his former lover.

Blake pulled a chair out for the heavily pregnant Stephanie and she slipped into it.

Tya knew she was staring but she could not take her gaze of the spectacle before her.

Blake sat in the chair opposite Stephanie, but even from this distance he didn't look settled.

In fact, Tya thought he would jump up and flee any minute.

She couldn't hear them, but from their expression and body language she guessed they were arguing.

Tya had lost her appetite so she put the lid on the salad, but she was afraid to move from her seat in case she was seen.

Stephanie leaned forward and talked animatedly to Blake.

CHAPTER 7

"I'm sorry Connor hassled you," Stephanie said.

Blake leaned back in his chair needing whatever minute distance he could get. "Obviously he's keen for the child to be mine and he's not happy about the tests. I am happy taking responsibility."

"But what about us?"

"There is no us, Stephanie."

"But Blake, I still love you."

"Well, that's unfortunate for you, Steph. You should've thought about that before you let Connor into your pants."

Stephanie reached out and placed her hand on his. "I'm so sorry Blake. I was confused, and terrified of the huge step I was taking."

"Was it the only time—on that day?"

A dark shadow flitted across her expression and her mouth tightened slightly. Blake didn't need her answer.

"It just happened, Blake, I was so vulnerable, and Connor comforted me and well..."

"Liar."

She flushed an ugly red. "You were angry at me for turning your partnership down..."

"Don't. Just don't. If it was just the one time there would be no question whose baby it is."

Tears glistened in her eyes.

"You shouldn't have been unfaithful. I loved you. I was never unfaithful in thought or deed. For Christ's sake wasn't I enough in bed for you."

Tears filled her eyes and trickled down her cheeks. "I'm sorry."

"I don't think sorry covers it, Steph."

She gazed up into his eyes. "But what about our baby? Don't you want to be a father to him?"

Blake almost choked on the air he breathed as an invisible noose tightened around his neck and strangled his soul. "I have to think about it. *If* he's mine then I'll have to consider my options."

"*If he's yours?* For God's sake, Blake."

Blake shrugged ignoring the touch of roughness in Stephanie's tone. Defensive almost. "As I said, if he's mine, I will consider my options."

"And what about *us?*"

"*Us,* Stephanie? There is never going to be an us, again. You blew your chances."

"Blake."

"Why didn't you marry Connor?"

"He didn't ask me, besides Connor is... lacks..."

"You mean he's good looking enough for a quick intimate encounter from time to time, but not relationship material—no money, little education, no heritage or credentials where I possess all that's required by an ambitious social climber like you."

"Blake, it's not like that at all. Please say you'll forgive me. I want us to be a family."

"There's no chance of that. I'll support the kid if he's mine, but nothing more."

"So, you really have fallen for that other woman."

Blake shook his head. "That's not the reason, Stephanie. I don't love you anymore. You ripped my heart to shreds on our wedding day. And it wasn't the first time you had manhandled our love. Choosing to go to Hector and Hector over my practice cut deep."

Stephanie shrugged. "It was personal benefit Blake. You were just growing your practice so not much on offer at the time. I wanted more and Hector and Hector offered the prestige you didn't. I didn't think it would matter so much to you. You're not the ambitious type."

"Was that why you took up with Connor?"

Stephanie smiled. "No Blake."

"Then why?"

Stephanie frowned. "That's water under the bridge Blake. So, what's she got that's so special. Is she better in bed or don't you remember how good it was between us? We were smoking hot."

The full thump of her betrayal smacked him in the ribs. The smoldering embers of hurt and anger flared into life. He leaned across the table close enough to smell her perfume. It turned his stomach. "If we were so good Stephanie why the hell did you need to try someone else?"

"I don't know Blake. I regret it I really do."

"Yeah so do I, well at least I did."

"So, are you going to marry this other woman?"

Her question stabbed at him. He glared at the woman in front of him-the one who had hurt him, shattered him, and stolen his ability to trust. He deeply resented her question.

"It's none of you bloody business, Stephanie whether I marry Tya or not."

"Well, I may not want her as stepmother to my son. I'll cause you trouble, Blake."

If Blake had been a violent man, he would have slapped her, then, right there in public, but he would never hit a woman, or probably a man for that matter. Violence provided pain not answers. But hell, he was mad enough to lose all restraint. He needed to get away. He jerked free of the chair and leaned on the table his knuckles white as they clenched into fists against the wooden tabletop.

"Be warned, Stephanie. Stay out of my life. Leave Tya alone or you will regret it sorely."

She glared up at him. Defiance glittered green in her hazel eyes.

Fiery ire flashed through him. "I have very powerful allies Stephanie, and I will use them."

"You would hurt your son's mother?"

Her words slapped at him. Could he hurt her and therefore hurt the child? He didn't know if he could, but he damn well wasn't going to let her know that. "Just try me and see. It could be a very fast way to lose your child altogether."

She jerked back from his growled threat. "You wouldn't."

"Do you want to risk it?"

"Blake," she wailed.

He ignored her, turned with a savage jerk and stalked across the food court.

Out of the corner of his eye something familiar caught his attention. He turned and saw her. His insides shrank into a tortured bundle. Tya. *Oh, hell she had seen him with Stephanie.* It wouldn't look good and cause her to question his honesty.

He looked back at Stephanie. He couldn't see her expression because she had her face buried in her hands.

He sighed and turned back to Tya. The table was empty. He glanced around in between the milling people. She was gone. A stone of dread settled in his chest. He needed no explanation of how she was thinking. Her vanishing act said it all. She had it all so wrong. An urgent need to find her and put it right poked at him.

He looked at the time. She could be anywhere. He would have to go to the garden or her house and wait. Damn it the longer he delayed correcting her perception of the issues the worse she would see him and probably the less she would believe him. He messaged. No response.

For the first time he now dreaded the return of the DNA results. If the unborn baby turned out to be his as he expected, it would do nothing for his desire to win Tya over. For whatever reasons she was reluctant to get involved and having a newborn son would only strengthen her arguments against him. Her assurances that she was not good enough also worried him. He could think of nothing that would make that assertion true.

His commitment to a meeting with a couple of contactors regarding the development on the outskirts of the CBD had him chaffing at the bit and he struggled to make himself settle enough to put forward a good set of responses to the questions.

When he finally escaped from the formalities he drove straight to the garden. Only to find it deserted. All the ground was black and wet, rain dripping from every leaf. He climbed back in the car and roared around the corner to her house. He jumped out of the car and bashed on her door. No answer.

He sat in the rickety chair on the verandah for a long time his arms hanging down over the sides. He clenched and unclenched his fists in between pointlessly checking his phone.

The soft creak of the gate and tentative footsteps alerted Blake. He pulled back into the shadows and tensed into stillness as a woman stopped by the letterbox. Blake guessed she hadn't seen him in the gloom blanketing the verandah. She appeared about forty, dressed like a sex worker from the streets. The mail box lid clunked as she flicked it open and dragged the mail out. After shuffling through them she stuffed them back in the box. Without shutting the lid the woman ambled up the path with a swagger of ownership and stepped up onto the verandah.

"What do you want?"

The woman jumped and spun around at Blake's quiet question. Heavily made up she looked even more like a working girl close up than she had before.

"And who are you to be asking?" she snapped back.

"I'm a friend of Tya's."

"Whoooohoo so she has posh friends these days. Well, I outrank you, fella, flash and all as you might be. I'm her mother."

Blake struggled to hold his mouth shut as his jaw sagged. *Her mother. It can't be.* "And you have proof of that then?"

The woman cackled. "Don't you think the likeness is enough?"

Blake wanted to wipe his eyes and banish the vision, but instead he stared at the wretch in front of him. God damn it he could see a likeness. "No, I don't see it."

She laughed louder and shrugged her thin shoulders. "Huh just don't want ta see it. Can't blame ya. Well, I'll scoot then. Tell Tya, her mum called past, and I'll be back."

Blake couldn't form a response as he watched the woman stroll down the garden path and out the gate.

Once on the footpath she paused just a moment, gave a slight wave, then disappeared.

Blake sagged back in the seat his energy seeped out with his incredulity. His mind refused to comprehend and reconcile that woman with the woman he loved. The concept fizzed in his mind. Could this be the reason Tya tried to keep him at arm's length. His head throbbed as realization sank in bringing understanding with it.

A good half an hour later he heard Tya's quick steps up the path and not wanting to scare her he stood and went down the steps to meet her.

She stared up at him, her expression full of bruised misery.

"Go away, Blake."

"Tya, please listen to me. Hear me out."

"I saw you in the Central Market today with her. All very cozy. Showing a last minute interest in case its yours?"

"It is not confirmed yet, Tya."

"Does it matter?"

"Yes, it does."

"What does that mean, Blake? If he's yours, you three will make a sweet little happy family and if he's not, I can have a look in.

"No, that's not how it goes at all."

"Then you tell me how it goes, Blake. No, on second thoughts, I don't want to know. I don't need to know because there is nothing between us and never can be."

"I'm going to tell you, Tya, whether you want to hear it or not. I deserve at least that much, don't I?"

She pushed past him and unlocked the door. "I don't know what you deserve, Blake, but it's not me, so there is no point listening."

He touched her arm.

She pulled away.

"Please just let me explain then I'll go if you still want me too."

She hesitated then pushed the door wide open. "In that case you'd better come in and I'll make some coffee."

Hope jumped inside his chest. She was at least going to listen to him. It was more than he had expected. He leaned against the bench and watched her brew the coffee. He didn't start his explanation until she handed him a mug and slid into the seat at the table. He seated himself opposite.

For a moment they sat in silence.

He stared into his coffee, not sure where to start petrified that with one wrong word she would chuck him out without letting him finish.

Even with the tension between them he was aware of the beginnings of stiffness in his cock. His body ached with the need to hold her, to love her, but knowing it was just a male way to show her how much she meant to him he pushed the ache aside. For this moment he must try the female way. Talking. Explaining.

"I know you're mad at me. Upset by what you saw, but if you will just let me explain."

She sipped her coffee, put the mug down and looked directly at him. "Well, I'm listening."

He cleared his throat. "I went into the city today for a business meeting and bumped into Stephanie. She was dropping some documents at the firm for her boss. She insisted I talk with her. She's angry that I have demanded DNA tests and that Connor is doing the DNA test as well. She wants the baby to be mine, not Connor's, because Connor is *not suitable*."

He paused to gather his thoughts.

"And."

"She tried to convince me that if the baby is mine, we should get back together and make a family. She tried to explain away the past, why she cheated, and make me understand how sorry she is."

Tya sipped her coffee but did not take her gaze from him.

Blake felt pinioned by her look, and the judgment in her eyes. He wanted it gone. He wanted to see the soft blue violet reflections in her eyes that showed in the throes of passion.

"I said no."

"Do you still love her?"

With a certainty that had grown even stronger today he shook his head. "No, I don't love her anymore."

"And what about the baby? Will you love him?"

Blake shook his head frowning. "I don't know how I'll feel if he's mine. I will support him financially, but as to anything else I don't know."

He cringed away from revealing Stephanie's threats. It was probably all talk anyway. He put his coffee cup down as he prevaricated whether to say something about the woman claiming to be her mother. If she was, it would explain Tya's reluctance to get involved. Did it matter to him? His breath caught in his chest and his heart skipped a couple of beats. His mind and his heart bounced against each other as the realization firmed in his mind that it didn't matter to him.

He rose and walked around the table. He held out his hands. "Please, Tya, give me a chance. I've fallen in love with you."

"You can't."

"I have."

She shook her head. "Blake, no."

He squeezed her hands. "Tell me you're not interested, even a little bit. Look me in the eyes and tell me you don't want me." He stared down at her and waited.

Tya swallowed hard. She stared up at him. Tears stung at the back of her eyes. She blinked and tore her gaze away from his. She shook her head. "I can't," she croaked.

"I knew it, and in that case, I intend to make the most of it. Keep in mind everyday that I am not going to stop trying to win your heart." He scooped her up in his arms and carried her to the bedroom and planted her in the middle of the bed.

She lay there watching him as he stripped.

There was nothing sensuous about it. He wanted her. His cock was hard and aching with a need to be satisfied.

He didn't even wait to undress her just pulled her knickers off and lifted her skirts.

Tya chuckled and wrapped her hands around his neck and pulled him on top of her. He immediately rolled over taking her with him and she found herself lying on top of him his swollen manhood very evident between them.

Tya wanted him. She was ready for him so she reached down and with very little movement guided him into her, rocking back and forth on her knees as he thrust with fast little thrusts.

She settled on his cock and snatched up her dress and dragged it over her head. With one hand he reached up and stroked her clitoris in gentle but swift circles while his other hand massaged her breasts flicking his thumb back and forth across her nipple. The passion exploded inside her as she felt his member stretching her each time he sank deep inside. They moved in rhythm, his cock, her hips and his fingers. Pleasure rushed through her from toes to fingertips then exploded in a fiery spray of intense pleasure from her nether regions right through to her head. She bit down hard on the cries that caught in her throat, wave after wave of sensation flooded over her as Blake thrust deeper and faster.

Moments later he groaned his release and thrust deep inside her. He stayed still for a long moment before his hips collapsed to the bed.

Tya slid partially off him to the bed leaving one leg trailing over his hips.

They lay in silence for quite a while. As Blake's breathing eased, he turned to her and looked down into her eyes. "I want to keep doing this forever. Will you let me?"

Tya shook her head.

He saw the glint of tears in her eyes. "Tell me, Tya. Tell me why you can't be mine."

She shook her head. "I can't tell you Blake, not yet."

"Whatever it is it doesn't matter," he murmured.

"It will. It does," she whispered back.

He lay his head on her breast. He wanted to tell her he'd met her mother, but he didn't want to destroy the warm glow between them. He needed her to tell him in her own time. He would not force the secret out of her.

It was the only thing interfering with his utter contentment. After months of self-imposed celibacy consumed with bitterness and anger, suddenly, unexpectedly, Tya had captured his heart. He wanted this woman like he had never wanted any other, and her rejection cut him to the core. He wasn't accustomed to women turning him down, but it wasn't his ego that hurt, it was his heart. She had rejected him claiming she was no good for him—for anyone. Blake had toyed with the idea of doing a background check, but immediately discarded it—he knew it wasn't right to pry just because he had the resources

CHAPTER 8

The sunset faded on the horizon coloring the air around them with a hazy gold.

Blake held her hand across the table stroking his fingers across her palm. He kept smiling at her. A sexy lazy smile that said all that needed to be said.

So absorbed in each other they hadn't taken the slightest bit of notice of their dining companions.

"Ah, Blake, such a shock to see you are still with her. Obviously, you don't know."

Tya shuddered as both the words and the scratchy high-pitched voice shattered the quiet and stabbed into her mind.

They looked up in unison as Stephanie waltzed down the balcony toward them a glass of wine in her hand.

Tya cringed as the woman approached and snuck a peep at Blake.

His contorted expression darkened; his grey eyes swirled with dark stormy shadows. He watched Stephanie approach. He snapped a glance at Tya, flashed a smile that barely made an impression on the chiseled planes of his face. "Don't worry. I'll give her short shift."

Animosity sparked from the heavily pregnant woman.

Tya squirmed in her seat, scrunching the serviette into crumpled ball before releasing it and scrunching again. Tya quickly cased the room for an escape route, almost rose to her feet, but dropped back as Blake growled.

"Go back to your table, Stephanie and stop guzzling wine, you're pregnant."

"You really think so." Stephanie stroked her baby bump and took another sip of wine. "I'll go when I've said what needs to be said. Darling, there are things you should know about, Ms. Tya Morley. I have been doing some research and I don't think you would want your reputation dragged through the mud. I doubt even your father will approve your little liaison." Her voice rang out across the now silent dining room.

All eyes were pinioned on the three of them.

Fear stabbed through Tya. Nausea roiled in her belly as she contemplated her exposure. *Not this way. Oh God I should have told Blake before we fell into bed together.*

Stephanie would sprout her information in the grubbiest way possible. And the inevitable would happen. Blake would back off. Not that they had a future anyway, but Tya would have enjoyed some more time to be romanced and loved. She fought down the bile that burnt in her chest.

"Just going to the ladies," Tya muttered as she scrambled out of her chair and skittered between the tables. Her heart beat in an uneven staccato beat, her lungs refused to breathe in air. Darting needles of panic prickled inside as anguish tightened as her make believe world collapsed. She pictured the look of disgust dawning in Blake's expression. Sobs battered her ribs. She swayed and staggered to the basin clutching the cold hard enamel to keep herself upright. Her reflection showed white in the mirror in the brightly lit ladies' room. *What have I got myself into? For goodness sake I know better than to get involved. Damn it.*

"You can't escape me by scuttling in here."

Tya glared at Stephanie. "What do you want from me?"

"I thought Blake deserved the truth. Do you think he would have bedded you if he knew you were a whore?"

"I'm not a whore."

"The apple never falls far from the tree, I say. Daughter like mother. She has quite a rap sheet for solicitation, drug possession, and disorderly conduct. And as for your brother well what can one say. You know a drug addict killed his mother, don't you?"

"Leave my mother out of this, and his for that matter. This is between you and me."

Stephanie laughed a sharp piercing crack. "You know he's having DNA tests done as soon as the baby is born, don't you?"

Tya nodded. She swallowed hard but the lump in her throat refused to move.

Stephanie moved closer, smiling. "And when the results come back that Stephen is his son and he sees his dear little face and holds him to his chest, do you think you'll have a chance then? He's not going to sacrifice fatherhood for someone like you."

"I wasn't asking him too. Regardless of the outcome he's not going to come back to you."

Stephanie cackled. "Really. Blake still has feelings for me. In fact, I think he still loves me. Anyway, it will all change when the baby arrives."

Tya stood straighter and gasped in air. "Then he's a bloody fool and not the man I think he is."

"Tya, Tya, even if he does not love me, he's not going to get himself involved with someone like you, especially now he knows your sordid background."

She stared at Stephanie. "Why do this and in public. I wear the shame everyday but there was no need to besmirch Blake's reputation."

Stephanie laughed. "Poor little, Tya. You shouldn't keep secrets."

"I've never done anything to hurt you. You ruined your own relationship with Blake."

Again, Stephanie laughed. Her wine spilled over the lip of the glass and sloshed on the floor. "You've taken my man. Look at him all gooey and lovesick over a whore's daughter when he should be holding my hand and whispering sweet nothings. Excited about his child's birth."

Suddenly Blake was there. "I'm never going to whisper sweet nothings in your ear, Stephanie, and when you've finished calling people whores consider your own behavior."

"Blake, darling." Stephanie threw herself at Blake, wrapped her hands around his neck and slammed her mouth against his.

Tya shook with a mixture of rage and humiliation.

"Get off me," Blake bellowed pushing Stephanie away.

She tottered slightly, the clatter of her heels loud on the tiled floor. "Blake."

Tya cringed against the inevitable even as Blake wrapped his arm around her shoulders and guided her out of the restroom.

Stephanie followed and grabbed at Blake's coat. She missed. Her glass smashed on the floor.

Blake shoved the restroom door open and eased Tya through and back into the restaurant.

"We'll leave, Tya, I don't like the company."

Stephanie slammed the door open and followed them.

"I wasn't finished with you, Tya," Stephanie screeched. "But Blake can hear the worst of it right now. "She waved her hand in the air. "Everyone can hear."

Shudders of trepidation rolled through Tya.

Every dining room occupant sat still, waiting for the confrontation and perhaps to glean a few words of juicy gossip.

Blake looked down at her and tightened his hold. "It's okay, Tya, nothing she can say will change the way I feel."

Tya shook her head, tears spilling from her eyes and sliding unattended down her cheeks. "Yes, she can and yes, it will."

Blake turned away and looked back at Stephanie. "What the bloody hell are you on about."

"She's the daughter of Evaline Morley, prostitute, addict and mother of two jailbirds and one an ice addict. You know what ice addict's do, don't you, Blake? They kill. And not only that she's sister to the notorious Toby Denton. How's that for a reference. It'll kill your father to know the depths you've sunk to Blake, darling."

Stephanie's words lashed at Tya. Humiliation burned through her. She tore herself from Blake's protective arm, pushed passed the gloating woman and ran.

"Tya."

She heard him call but didn't stop. She heard Stephanie's drunken cackling, and moved faster. The ever present shame whipped at her, gouging searing lumps from her heart and soul. Everyone had heard. Every diner. But the only one she cared about was Blake. Poor Blake. He must be gutted and shamed to find out in such a way who he had been associating with. She had never meant to fall in love with this man or hurt him in this way.

She cursed her folly. Cursed the fact she had broken her own rules. God help her now. She would have to move on. She couldn't bear the whispering from behind hands and the sideways looks in her direction.

She hurried down the ramp along the dark side of the shopping center, and out into the poorly lit back streets. She walked, ran and walked again. Her breath caught in ragged puffs. She glanced over her shoulder, but no one followed. She hadn't expected him too. Why would he come, after Stephanie had regaled him with her murky background? Besides, she wondered if deep down Blake still felt something for Stephanie.

She let herself into the house, but it reeked of him. She glanced in the bedroom, the site of their lovemaking; the echoes of their passion mocked her. She cried out, turned and fled. She didn't slow until she reached Thistle Street. The gate opened on a sad squeak, and she slipped between the plants and into the deep blackness of the unlit garden almost as dark as the shadows on her soul.

The tinkle of water called her and she sank exhausted onto one of the seats by the pond. There was no moon and very few stars out yet. She hunched with her knees up into the corner of the chair and stared at the pond. Tears tickled down her cheeks. She sniffed but didn't wipe them away. Almost with comprehension the darkness silvered in the subtle light from the moon as it rose huge and glowing above the fence.

She tensed. A whisper of sound ripped the silence apart. Someone was here. Had he followed her? Would he demand an explanation? Would she see the revulsion on his face? Nausea washed through her. She turned.

"So, this is where you hide when life kicks your arse."

Fatigue gripped her. She was not in the mood to deal with her mother. She could see she was in withdrawal. Even in the gloom she could see her shaking hands and the manic glint in her eyes.

"Go away, Mum. I don't have anything for you."

"I need money."

"I don't have any and if I did, I wouldn't give it to you." Tya waved at the garden. 'If you're hungry there's plenty of food, help yourself."

"Bugga food. It's not what I need. For God's sake, Tya, take pity on me. I need a fix, now."

Tya stood and faced her mother. "Take pity on you. I don't think so. What about the poor little bub in your belly. That I can have pity for."

Her mum sidled closer.

Tya tensed. This was not a good place to be baled up by her drug crazed parent. Tya watched her. She backed up. Hard against a solid body.

Hands groped at her and dragged her small handbag from her shoulder.

It caught in her elbow. She cried out and snatched the strap with her other hand.

"Get it, Kyle, drag it off her."

She glanced over her shoulder. "No, Kyle. Don't do this to me. I'm your sister. I can help you."

A bark of laughter cracked in her ears and even as she clung to the strap it slipped through her fingers.

"Sorry, sis. Mum needs some stuff."

She turned back. Her mother was right there. Tya never registered the hand as it slashed through the air. The sting of skin on skin shocked her. Tya tried to cry, to scream. Her mouth worked but no sound came out. The second slap jerked her head to the side.

"Mum," she wailed.

"I said I would teach you to be miserly with your one and only mother. Be grateful this is all you're getting. Next time it might be worse."

The plants in front of her shook and rattled. Blake burst out of the greenery shovel held high above his head.

"Oi who do think you are?" her mother shouted throwing her hands up over her head and backing away from Tya.

"I'm her knight in shining armor. Now skedaddle before I cave your bloody drug addled head in. Go on get going." Blake marched forward.

Evalina Morley backed away.

Kyle let go of Tya.

Her shaking legs gave way, and she collapsed to the ground.

Blake stood over her. "Go on, buzz off. Scum of the earth."

Evalina cackled. "If we are the scum then she," she pointed at Tya. "Is the flotsam and jetsam."

"Tya, would never be that no matter her background." Blake roared as he waved the shovel.

Her mum and brother disappeared at a run through the tomato bushes and Tya heard the rattle of the back fence as they left through the damaged gates.

She shut her eyes and dropped her head, unable to face him. He had seen the worst of what she had to offer. Her horrid criminal family. A cold lump of misery churned in her stomach while her heart tapped unevenly behind her breast. There was nothing to do, or say now, but for him to leave.

His hand was warm on her shoulder. "Up you get, Tya. Did they hurt you?"

She shook her head but made no effort to rise.

"Come on, up you get." He tried to lift her.

She made no effort to help him. "I should have told you," she murmured still keeping her head down. "I just wanted a short time to be loved and romanced. Just a small time."

"Maybe, but it wouldn't have made any difference."

She looked up now. "You still would have made love to me, knowing I'm a prostitute's daughter."

"Up," he said.

Tya allowed him to lift her to her feet.

"Now you listen here, and you listen good, Tya Morley. What your mother is, or isn't, makes no difference. It's you I want. It's you I love."

"But I'm no good, Blake. No good for anyone. I'm damaged goods—rotten to the core."

"Bullshit."

She shook her head at his denial. "The evidence is there—my father was a drunk, my uncle too. My mother's a drug addict and whore. Two of my brothers are in jail for violent offences and drug use and my younger brother, he's only fourteen, and already smoking, drinking and maybe even doing drugs."

"So..."

"So, I have bad blood, Blake. It's only a matter of time..."

"Bullshit," he said again and scooped her up into his arms. "My God, you're trembling. Let's get you home and warmed up."

He carried her up Thistle Street and around the corner. He wasn't even struggling when he set her down in front of her own front door.

"Keys."

"You're going to regret this, Blake Gifford. I'll only hurt you in the end. There is no happy ending for me."

"Shhhhh. Inside." Blake gave her a gentle guiding push. She crossed the threshold. Blake turned the light on in the hall. "Go." He pressed against her shoulder until she stepped forward. Both hands descended onto her shoulders and he swiveled her around and guided her into the bedroom.

"Into bed. I'll make some tea.

She stumbled to her tall boy."

Blake came back from the door and took her hands away from the drawers. "Into bed – no need for PJ's cos I am only going to take them off again."

A slightly hysterical giggle bubbled up. "I thought you needed the challenge."

He laughed as he headed for the kitchen.

Tya lay in the bed, clutching the quilt up to her chin unable to stop shivering. She felt drained. That was not the first time her mother had been violent but Kyle had always been civil enough. Her need must be desperate and her little brother following in her footsteps.

She struggled with Blake's acceptance of her background. It might be all right now in the throes of first love, but what of later. She had to make him understand she was no good for him.

When he returned, he had two cups of hot sweet tea and some buttered toast. He perched on the bed beside her and shared the supper with her.

"Blake, you should go. I'm not the right woman for you. You have to listen to me."

"No, I don't."

"Look at my mother. Not a maternal bone in her body. So unable to love, driven only by her next fix. Do you want to risk that? I don't believe I can be a good mother. I have no maternal instincts, with addiction baying for my blood. What if I slip, what if I give in. Do you want that?"

He took her cup and laid his fingers on her lips. "Shhh. You're not your mother and unlikely to turn into your mother. Now lay back I'm going to ravish you, slowly and thoroughly..."

"But your reputation? Your career will be ruined and politics. You will never be able to go into politics."

His lips silenced her protests.

She vowed to try again to dissuade him. Later, after he had ravished her.

She pushed his shirt apart to expose the broad expanse of his hard, muscular chest with its light sprinkling of hair that trailed down to the band of his trousers. She reached up and ran her hands over the satiny smooth skin. He leaned away for a moment then the room was lit with a soft glow.

"I like to see," he said quietly.

"So do I," she whispered as she climbed to her knees with her hands exploring the golden satin of his skin as the candlelight flickered over its curves and dips. She leaned forward and kissed his shoulders, tasting him for the first time. Her pussy clenched aching with such a strong need she was almost squirming. She kissed him again, easing lower each time her lips touched his skin until she found his nipples. She nipped at them, and he flinched even as he groaned. She could feel his cock pressing against her belly straining to be released. She went to undo his trousers.

He stopped her intention instead he guided her hands to his buttocks then reached up and cupped both her breasts and lifted them slightly so he could suckle.

As he took the first nipple in his mouth she almost screamed as her pussy convulsed in ecstasy. Her flesh already soft, hot and wet. She needed him so badly.

He slipped her bra off and with a lithe movement he removed her knickers.

She knelt naked before him.

He gazed at her as he ran his hands ever so lightly over her silken smooth skin. 'You are so beautiful Tya—so perfect.'

'Take me, Blake, please take me now.' Even as she begged she undid his pants.

When they finally fell away from his slim hips he stepped out of them. His cock rose up from its nest of hair, smooth, hard and throbbing.

She cupped his balls then slid her hand up the length of his shaft. It was thick and long topped with a satin smooth nob already glistening with moisture in the candle glow. She trailed her finger over the tip.

His cock danced.

"Take me, Blake."

He eased her back on the back and climbed in beside her. "Are you sure, Tya?"

"For God's sake Blake," she muttered as she parted her legs.

He caressed her once with his fingers then eased himself on top of her.

She guided him. The moment his cock touched the outside of her pussy she felt the spasms begin and she bucked her hips.

He caught her urgency then, her need and plunged his cock deep, withdrew and plunged again and again.

Tya felt it penetrate, stretching her, mixing liquid fire with liquid fire. She cried out and her body convulsed and shuddered under his assault. She clawed his back as she rose to meet his savage thrusts. 'More, Blake, more,' she cried out against his mouth.

He increased his tempo and thrust harder and deeper.

She gasped for breath but almost cried out as the spasms faded. She reached down between the sweat glossed bodies and found her clit. She rubbed it now with a desperate rhythm. Almost immediately she felt her body's tension gather. She moved her hand in time with Blake thrusts. A delicious rhythm pulsing to a crescendo.

He was sinking deeper now, so deep it almost felt too much.

Her whole body sizzled, twitched and throbbed. She squeezed her legs tightly around Blake's hips and met him thrust for thrust. Her whole body trembled and convulsed, and her orgasm exploded, tightening her muscles around his cock, as her body throbbed with exquisite pleasure. She thrust up and paused. Her cry choked back in her throat. Sweat poured from her body as she was sized again and again by the spasms. She was vaguely aware of Blake's groans and the throb of his cock pulsing against her electrified flesh with his release. She squeezed her muscles around it as he pumped hot fluid into her.

He groaned again and again before he collapsed onto her, his chest heaving.

She let him rest for a while in his own rapture his cock still in her as her body still shuddered faintly with aftershocks.

After a few moments he moved sluggishly and pulling her with him he rolled to his side. His chest still heaved and his eyes were closed but one hand remained possessively around her.

She lay on her back struggling to gain control of her breathing even while she enjoyed the small after pulses caressing her pussy.

***

As he held her cuddled into his side, he replayed the incident at the garden. Her family. To be cursed with such as that was unfair. Tya had obviously worked her way above and away from it all, but they would always be there to drag her down when she least expected it. A sliver of doubt wormed its way into his mind. Would it matter? To him? To his family or to others? Would it be cruel to Tya to drag her kicking and screaming into his social circle of lawyers and the wealthy elite? Would they spurn her if the secret ever came out? Did he have the right to do that to her?

Confusion swirled around him. He had thought about politics and he knew that if he had Tya in his life there would be no politics. He would never expose her to that.

"What you thinking?"

He sensed her concern in the tone of her voice.
"Not much."

"You haven't said much about my situation."

"Not much to say. You are you, and your family is a separate entity."

"But it won't be good for you. If you were going into politics in a couple of years I would ruin it for you."

Blake grunted his disapproval. "Maybe I don't want politics that badly after all."

"But, Blake, you said. But you need a good woman with a clean slate and an impeccable background."

"Or stay out of politics. Besides I have my father's company to manage."

"But you can't abandon your dreams—not for me."

He turned to look down into her eyes. With gentle fingers he caressed her lips. "Shhh, my love."

"No, Blake, this has to end. Now. Go and don't come back. I will not let you ruin your life for such as me."

"Tya, maybe my life will be ruined by not having you in it."

She sat up and glared down at him. "Rubbish. I'm just a passing phase for you. Now please go before I end up crying."

Hurt stabbed at him. He recognized the seriousness of her words in her expression. A little part of him wondered if she was right. But he wanted her so badly.

He let go of her and rolled out of bed. She sat there hunched up in the sheet. She couldn't look at him. He dressed slowly hoping she would suddenly change her mind, but she didn't.

"I'm going, Tya, for now, but this is not the end of it do you hear me."

"No, Blake, this is the end. I will destroy you if you stay."

"I don't really care about politics that much, Tya. I would rather have you."

"Go."

He left, her words scarring his heart and soul.

CHAPTER 9

Tya moved through the garden slowly, melancholy dragging at her soul. She had done the right thing sending him away, but it hurt. Did it hurt him as much? Would he come back? Part of her hoped so but the other part; the logical, practical side hoped he wouldn't. She didn't know if she had the strength to banish him again. Her whole body ached with despair.

With a sudden flash she decided that being in the garden alone was not good for her mood so she hurriedly finished up watering the seedlings, before washing her hands. Footsteps startled her. She looked up but saw no-one. She moved silently through the plants.

She stood by the pool, reading the plaque.

Tya hurried up behind her.

"What are up doing here? This is private property."

"You can talk, this land belongs to Blake."

"It does and we have his permission."

"For the time being but I'll see you removed when we are back together. When my precious baby is proven to be his son."

"That remains to be seen, but in the meantime, please remove yourself."

She waved a hand at the memorial. "This is his problem. Lost his mother, you know, when he was twelve. I don't think he has ever gotten over it."

"Maybe not, but that is his business how he grieves."

"True, but I can't understand why he's taken to you, a drug addict's daughter. You know it was a druggie that killed her."

Tya flinched. "Yes, I know."

"You know his father will never accept you, he has a perverse and justified hatred of drug addicts."

"I'm not a drug addict." Despite her protests Tya already accepted the truth in Stephanie's words.

Stephanie glowered. "It won't matter. And if he stays with you no-one will employ him in law. A lawyer has to have a clean slate so does a politician."

Anguish tore through Tya knowing the blame lay squarely with her.

"You know he will be socially ostracized while he has you hanging on his coat tails. Do you want that for him? If you loved him, you would send him away. Then again maybe you just want to use him to get out of your own quagmire. Maybe you don't really love him at all."

"I do love him. I have already told him to go and not come back."

Stephanie stared at her, raising her eyebrows. "Really. So, you do care."

"Yes, I care but just because I can't have him doesn't mean he will come back to you."

Stephanie threw her head back and laughed. A piercing, high pitched cackle. "Of course, he will." She stroked her belly. "When Stephen is proven to be his. Blake is a big softy and he would not want to see his son fatherless. We could even give Stephen a sibling."

Nausea washed over her. The thought of Blake making love to Stephanie punched her in the gut. She hauled in a deep breath and released it with a sigh. She had to stay calm. Hysterics was not the way to best this woman.

"And if your baby isn't his?"

"He is."

"Then why the need for tests?"

"Oh, shut up, whore. You need to take this to heart. Blake's reputation will be ruined. You, and only you, have the where-with-all to destroy. If you love him, you will stay the hell out of his life. If you don't, I'll see you both suffer the consequences."

"Was it you who spread the rumors?"

Stephanie gave an evil grimace turned and strolled away.

Tya sagged onto the chair. Poor Blake. Tears rolled down her cheeks. She stared at the rose bush. *Francis Gifford, your son needs you. Protect him. I love him but will not see him destroyed even if it breaks my heart.*

The breeze whispered through the blooms scattering the pink perfumed petals at her feet

***

He hadn't slept much when the phone buzzed. A woman's accented voice echoed as he accepted the call.

"Mr. Gifford?"

"Yes."

"Mr. Goren asked me to call and let you know he has cancelled your appointment for today. He is no longer interested in getting a quote from you regarding the proposed heritage renovation to his offices."

"What? Why?"

But the caller had already disconnected.

Blake rolled over and put the phone back on the bedside table.

Nasty thoughts and suspicions rattled through his head. He had put a lot of work into preparing his proposal for Goren, Latimer and Smythe lawyers to renovate their heritage listed offices. It didn't take much for him to determine what had caused such a curt dismissal.

***

Fury drove him. He barged into the office of Hector, Hector and Huxtable. The receptionist peered up at him.

He didn't pause for her to greet him but strode toward Stephanie's office.

"You can't go in there, sir."

He ignored the desperate plea shouted at his back.

Her door was ajar.

He shoved it open.

She looked up.

"Ah, Blake how nice to see you."

"You conniving bitch. How dare you interfere in my life. What the hell did you say to Goren?"

"Nothing, Blake, darling. What is the matter?"

He strode forward and slammed his hands on the desk. Stephanie jumped.

"Liar. What did you offer your cousin to tell tales about me? Do you think this is going to change how I feel about you, about Tya?"

"But, Blake, I did no such thing. Are you getting a little paranoid?"

"Stay the hell out of my life."

"You know Tya doesn't want you. She told me she sent you away."

Her words sliced through him, dicing his fury into small pieces.

"She knows she's no good for you. A whore's daughter. Here, have a look. I have the rap sheet right here."

"I don't give a damn about her mother's rap sheet."

"You should, Blake, or there might be more like Goren."

Blake reined in his rage. He looked directly at her. "If you don't stay out of my life, you had better hope that wretched baby is not mine because if he is, I will make your life hell. Custody, access, visitation rights and never mind about maintenance. You will wish you'd never met me, let alone birthed my child. And leave Tya alone as well."

She swallowed. "She will destroy you."

He stood straight. "You destroyed me Stephanie with your unfaithfulness and lies. Tya has healed me in a way no other woman could and I tried plenty. Stay out of my life."

He turned and stalked out of her office. This time pulling the door shut with a loud thud. The receptionist eyed him warily. Blake ignored her. He suspected half the office had heard his rant. And sure enough, Clemet Hector appeared in his doorway. "Blake Gifford. Having a spot of bother, are we?"

Blake grimaced. "Not anymore, it's all sorted."

Clemet Hector nodded. "Good, I do not tolerate personal stoushes by my staff. I have high expectations and if not met th golden goose will be cooked. "

Blake stalked passed him, not breathing freely until he exited the building.

He desperately wanted to see Tya, to hold her, love her, and tell her it would be all right, but he needed to calm down. He needed to know if the child was his.

***

Despite the constant need for Tya, that ate away at him, he stayed away from the garden and buried himself in his father's company. He waited impatiently and apprehensively for the baby to arrive and be tested. He owed it to Tya and himself to sort this ugly tangle out. He had to know how he would feel if the child was his. Not that it was going to change how he felt about Stephanie or Tya. He got up early, ran, dressed and went to either the office or the sites currently under construction.

By the end of the week, he was exhausted. He settled down early for another sleepless night, his mind refusing to shut down as a multitude of thoughts bashed around in his head.

Nevertheless he groaned when his phone clattered on the bedside table at two am. He groaned rolled over and picked it up. He read the message. The contents spearing through him.

Taking Stephanie to hospital she's in labor. If you want to see your son born you better come now to Women's and Children's. When its proven yours, you'll regret not being here.

He dragged his hand through his tousled hair. His chest tightened and his stomach churned. He wanted to throw the phone away from him. To un-see the text. Would he regret it? Nausea washed over him. He did not want to see Stephanie, to observe her pain, and effort to give birth. It would be too intimate considering how he felt and he was beyond offering her sympathy or support.

He scrambled out of bed and paced the room. He went to stare out the window at the dark sky with the silvery moon floating just above the horizon leaving a silvery trail across the stillness of the ocean. *Holy shit. What should he do? Would he regret it? Maybe. But what if the child was not his? Did he want to expose himself to that type of emotion. He had always considered birth as a miracle. Something special the parents shared together. But he didn't want to share this with Stephanie.* He paced back and forth, then flopped on the bed. He wasn't going. He couldn't face it. And he couldn't bear the thought of Stephanie's smug expression. Hell, he was pilloried if he did or didn't.

He rolled over and stared at the ceiling. The phone rattled again. He stared at the text.

You're not coming, are you? You gutless bastard leaving Steph to give birth to your son ALONE. You'll regret this.

The words burned into his brain. He switched the phone off and dumped it into the top drawer. He lay there with his eyes closed but sleep evaded him until it was light outside. Then he pulled the quilt over his head and finally drifted into a restless slumber.

It was well past noon when he woke. He showered, dressed and wandered to the kitchen to get a coffee and something to eat. Alice was preparing lunch. He sat in the chair next to his father.

"Wondered when you would surface son. Bad night?"

Blaske pulled the phone out of his pocket. "Yep. Talisha messaged me that Stephanie was in labor." He turned the phone on. There was a barrage of texts. Most from Talisha berating him for not coming. Then a photo of Stephanie and the baby. Then a close up of the little boy. Blake's heart sank. He was cute and he could be his son. He handed the phone to his father.

His father glanced at the photo then without comment handed the phone to Alice.

She glanced at it then passed it to Rhiana as she wandered in and pulled up a chair.

Rhianna looked at the photos. "Cute kid." She looked across at Blake. "Will they do the tests soon. I don't want to get attached unless it's yours."

Blake took the phone and typed a short message to both Talisha and Stepahanie.

Congratulations on the safe arrival of Stephen. Glad it went well. Get the tests done asap. Then he closed the cover and put it on the table. "Yeah, that's how I feel along with the guilt, hurt and frustration. It should have been mine without any doubts and that's what hurts, the betrayal and the doubt."

Over the next few days Talisha and Stephanie bombarded his phone with pictures until finally unable to stand the pressure he blocked both their numbers.

***

A week later he had a call from the medical specialist's rooms. The results of the tests were all back. The receptionist would not give them out over the phone and insisted that all three interested parties be at a ten am appointment tomorrow.

***

The following morning, he met Connor, and Stephanie, at the clinic. Trepidation thundered in his heart. The outcome could change his life forever. He knew Stephanie would put pressure on him to renew their relationship when it was confirmed Stephen was his and although he knew kids did better with a proper family, he also knew they could never be that. He didn't love or trust her. In fact, he despised her. He dreaded the thought of the child being his, with a mother like that.

Connor looked relaxed as he lounged back in his chair.

Blake had to steel himself to enter the room and take the few steps it needed to bring him to the desk.

Stephanie sat stiff and unmoving in the second chair, her head held high, and her expression defiant. She had left the baby with someone and Blake thought this was a good thing. Poor little mite was too young to be affected by adults scrabbling over his ownership, but Blake knew he would have felt uncomfortable. Stephanie glared at him, her hands clasped in her lap.

"Hi, mate. Ready for the big reveal," Connor asked.

Blake frowned. "No need to sound so cheerful about casting a child aside."

"Awww, he'll get over it, don't you reckon?"

"Actually, I haven't thought about it."

"Yeah, Stephanie told me you've got yourself a bit of floozy in tow. Keeping you distracted from the main business then?"

Connor's words stabbed at him. Ire rose in a burning acid flow into his chest. He clenched his fists but held them tightly by his side. "Watch your mouth, Connor. Tya is not a floozy and she has nothing to do with this business."

"Sorry to offend. Only going on what she told me."

"You should know better than that, Connor. It's what brought you here."

Connor spluttered and coughed. "Too true mate, too true."

The doctor entered and took his seat. He glanced over them and gave a slight nod of greeting.

"I have the results here." He opened the envelope and unfolded the sheet of paper.

"Hurry it up, mate, I have things to do," Connor urged.

The doctor frowned in his direction. "A little patience, Mr. MacGregor."

Connor sat back in his seat with a nod.

"I have examined the results and the conclusion is that you, Mr. MacGregor, and the child known as Stephen Sabik are not biologically related."

Stephanie made a slight choking sound. Then she smiled across at Blake.

Blake's throat clenched; icy disbelief rushed through him. *He's mine.* He glared at her. "I meant what I said, so don't gloat."

Her smile faded.

"I'm off the hook. Sorry, mate," Connor crowed stroking his beard and flicking his dreadlocks back over his shoulder.

Blake grimaced at Connor.

"And in line with your claim Mr. Gifford you are also not the biological father of said child."

Blake's little remaining energy seeped out and he sagged against the wall. He would have sunk to the floor if not for the solid obstacle pressed against his back. Blake's stomach turned and clenched as if punched. Nausea washed over him as the meaning of the doctor's statement sank in. He was not Stephen's father, but nor was Connor. The ramifications for Stephen were terrible.

Stephanie whimpered.

Blake struggled to speak. He swallowed and cleared his throat. "For God's sake, Stephanie how many others were there? No, don't answer. I don't think I want to know."

"What about Stephen?" she wailed.

Connor glared at Stephanie. "God damn it, Steph, you should have thought about that when you decided to bed hop."

"I loved you, Connor."

Connor leapt forward, grabbed Stephanie's shoulders and hauled her out of the chair. "You bloody cheating bitch. Nothing more than a whore."

She sobbed louder, keeping her head down.

Blake pushed away from the wall not at all sure of his balance, but not willing to allow Connor to rough

Stephanie up. "Ease up, Connor. Violence isn't going to help."

Connor glared at Blake, but he let go.

Stephanie sank back into the chair. "I'm sorry. I'm sorry," she spluttered through her tears.

Blake leaned on the back of the chair Connor had just vacated. *He's not mine. I'm free.* Free to love Tya. To have our own family with no complications. *If she'll have me.* He trembled, not sure if it was hurt, disgust or rage. He needed to get out of the room. Away from her, and him, and everything to do with his past.

He pushed himself upright took a few steps toward the door then turned. "Do you actually know who the father is Stephanie?"

She nodded. "Now I do and it's the worst result, but I can't say."

"Can't or won't say? Your poor child."

"Oh Blake, I'm sorry. I regret it so much. I did love you, but... but...I had ambitions."

Cold rage crackled through Blake. "Ambitions. So, who? Which one Hector, senior, Hector Junior or..."

She shook her head, tears sliding down her cheeks.

"Holy shit. You slept with Hector to get your partnership, didn't you? I knew you were good, but to rise so fast... Good grief, you slept with the old man. Good luck trying to claim child support from that one."

"I can't. Clemet will turf me into the street with no references, and blacklist me. I can't tell."

"You've made a bloody mess of things, Steph," Connor chortled close to her ear.

"Leave it, Connor."

"Well, she has."

"Yes, but think of the poor child." Blake said as he staggered across the room. He struggled with the door handle his fingers shaking and sweaty. It finally swung open and he blindly found his way to the car park. He looked around not sure where he'd even put his car. The clatter of footsteps behind him shredded what was left of his nerves. It was her. With a wrench through his distress, he located his car and strode towards it as fast as his shaking legs would carry him. The world spun in distorted clouds of grey and black. The pavement swayed under his feet.

"Blake, please wait. I want to explain."

He cringed at the sound of her voice. The audacity of her request ripped through him. He didn't want or need explanations. He wanted to get away. Far away.

His hand was on the door handle when she reached him. "Please, Blake, hear me out."

He turned to her, a multitude of angry words on his tongue. "I hope it has been worth it. And you called Tya a whore. God damn it, Stephanie, she makes fifty of you, in morals, looks, brains and scx appeal. Get away from me, and stay away, or I'll drop a line to Clemet."

Her face turned red, crumpled and fresh tears ran down her cheeks and dripped off the tip of her nose. "Blake."

She reached out to touch him, but he dodged out of her clasp, opened the door and slipped inside. He started the ignition and accelerated away. He glanced once in his mirror. Stephanie stood in the empty space, shoulders slumped, head bowed. A wave of nausea washed over him, but it couldn't annihilate the lump of disgust in his gut. The one he felt sorry for was the child.

He drove and drove along the esplanade, up the expressway and into the hills. He couldn't remember where

he'd been but slowly the horror of the morning slipped
from him. He noticed the blue sky, felt the heat of the
sun through the windscreen and a rumble of hunger in his
gut. He grabbed a sandwich and a cold drink and sat on
the bonnet of his car under a shady tree to eat. Finally letting the ramifications of the morning sink in he breathed
deeply letting calm wash over him. Calm, and peace, along
with a sense of freedom and lightness he hadn't felt in a
long time. It was time to head home. For the first time in
months home was the place he wanted to be.

Blake scurried up the stairs from the garage ignoring
the new lift his father had installed. He threw his jacket
in the hall, tore off his tie and unbuttoned the collar of
his shirt. There was a peace tinged with hope in his heart.
He paused. The house seemed quiet. Blake glanced in the
kitchen as he strode passed. No Alice. He went straight
onto his father's favorite spot by the big floor to ceiling
windows looking out over the sea. With the dread banished he was keen to share his news.

"Dad, how're you feeling?"

His dad looked up, deep lines etched across his forehead.
"Pretty good actually son, but I rest every day, on doctor's
orders. I've been waiting for you. How did it go?"

Blake sat on the edge of the chair opposite his father.
"The child's not mine, Dad."

"Bloody hell, so it's Connor's. That's decidedly unfortunate for the child."

Blake shrugged. "It is especially unfortunate as he is also
not Connor's."

"What the devil?"

Blake smiled at his father. "She admitted sleeping with
Clemet Hector to fast track herself to a partnership. She'll

have to choose between a father for her child or her newly minted partnership in the firm."

"Well, I never, Clemet Hector. Wouldn't have thought the old dog had it in him, but with Elizabeth now in a home with dementia I suppose he got lonely. Poor child."

Blake leaned back in his chair letting his father absorb this news first. He wanted to broach the subject of Tya. A lump of unease coiled in his gut and tightness gripped his throat. He didn't know what he would do if his father reacted negatively. Could he give up Tya?

He steepled his fingers and stared out at the view. The sea was choppy today. Little white scuds bounced over the bay pushed by a seaward breeze. The sun glinted on the water, highlighting the blue and greens.

"Something else on your mind, son? I hope you're not going to tell me you're backing out of the company. That you want to go back to law."

Blake glanced at his father then back out at the view. "Don't worry Dad, I'm not backing out of the company or going back to law. But there is something else I want to ask about."

"Well spit it out. Never does any man good to bottle things up."

Blake looked back at his father slightly amused at his father's changed perceptions. He would have been one of the worst at bottling things up before his heart attack. Obviously, the near-death experience had wrought more changes than curing his workaholic habits.

"I've met this woman," Blake said.

"I see. So, what's the problem?"

Blake shook his head not sure if he really wanted to do this, now he'd started. The words choked in his throat and tumbled in his mind.

"Out with it, Blake. There has to be a problem or you wouldn't be talking to me."

"It's not her, it's her family."

"Well, is it her, or the family, you're interested in? If something like that bothers you, she isn't the right woman for you."

Blake jumped out of the chair, icy surges of blood driving him forward as he paced across the room. He inhaled held the breath then let it out before he turned to his father. "It's my family I have doubts about Dad. You in particular. I don't want to have to choose."

"And what makes you think you'll have to?"

"Her mum is a prostitute and drug addict well known around the traps as Evalina Morley and two of her brothers are in goal one of them being Toby Denton. I remember his case because Hector was the defense lawyer. Tya has nothing to do with them and she is nothing like them. Her family are an unfortunate accident of birth, but I couldn't bear it if she got hurt or rejected by my family because of her background."

His father frowned. "I'm hurt, Blake that you ever thought for a moment this family would be so snobby."

"Dad, they're addicts...an addict killed Mum."

"Blake, I appreciate your concerns for me, but your mother's death was a long time ago. As long as the young woman concerned is not into such things. In that case I would then have trouble. Although with that background some of our social circle might be a little reluctant to include her."

"Tya does not do drugs, in fact she doesn't even smoke or drink. She lives in fear she might get addicted to some substance."

"Does this mean you're discarding the idea of going into politics? I don't think it would be wise to expose this woman to the cruelty of that scandal mongering."

Blake shrugged. "I wasn't really set on politics and to be honest I would rather have Tya than be prime minister. And besides I committed to the company now and I'd like to expand on my philanthropic activities. Tya already feeds a women's shelter and many of the battlers around the garden she made on the Thistle Street."

"Then there's no problem. When do we get to meet this young lady who has mended your heart?"

Blake snorted. "I don't know, Dad. She refuses to have me."

"What? Any woman in her right mind would snap you up."

Blake laughed out loud now. "I'm not the problem, Dad. She says she's not good enough – from the wrong side of the tracks and all that and she has a deep-seated shame about her family."

"Mmmm, she could be right, son. It might be a hard road to get acceptance by the fraternity but as you've sold your practice it won't matter. So if the going gets tough in your relationship you won't want to be throwing that at her."

"Funny, Tya said the same thing, but if my love turns out to be wrong then it will be my mistake not hers. You know what, Dad I don't give a damn what they think. All that worried me was you. I wanted your acceptance. I don't need anyone else's."

"Go get her then, son."

Blake smiled. "You don't know, Tya, Dad."

"Ah, but I know you, and she has mended your broken heart. What more could a father ask."

With his angst soothed by his father's reassurances Blake felt strong enough to overcome Tya's resistance. If his dad was okay with it then no-one else mattered. He headed for Tya's house. He knocked on the door.

She took a while to respond and greeted him with a frown. "I told you to go away, Blake. I'm not for you." She held the door partly closed.

"You are for me, Tya." Blake put a hand up on the door and pushed.

She resisted his pressure. "Go away."

"Tya, please." He pushed against the door again. "If you prefer we could just agree to enjoy each other's company without a long term goal."

"That's a recipe for hurt and you know it."

"I don't care. I've been hurt before and I've mended. I want you, Tya."

"Please don't do this."

"Yes, Tya. Say yes to me."

"I can't." She pushed the door closed.

He stood outside staring at the peeling door. *It needs painting.* He knocked. She did not return.

He leaned close to the door. "I'm not going away. I'll wait out here until you agree to see me."

He paced back and forth in the quiet of the verandah. She had to come out eventually. But what did he do then? Accost her. Force her to what... He slumped back in the old armchair. He didn't want to force her to do anything. He wanted her to come willingly into his arms and life and he didn't know how to overcome the barriers she had so firmly set in place.

***

Tya sat inside, straining to hear any sound from Blake. She wanted him so desperately but knew there would be too many sacrifices on his part. She couldn't guarantee not to become addicted to some substance, she had no maternal instincts but her greatest concern was his rejection by his peers. She couldn't possibly interfere with his desire to enter politics. *No, it is better this way.* Although tempted to take him on short term she already felt the tender fingers of love entwining her heart and they grew stronger each time she saw him. It had to stop.

She hadn't heard anything for a long time. The sun had dropped below the horizon and darkness wrapped tendrils around her house. The garden needed watering. She peeped out the window. He was still there asleep in the chair. She smiled. Tenderness swamped her. The urge to reach out and touch him shivered over her skin. To stroke his face, kiss him. Immediately her body responded with lightning quick sparks of desire.

She sighed as she picked up her work boots and headed out the back door. With a controlled tug Tya pulled the back door shut and walked gingerly in her socks around the side of the house. He still slept in the chair his man bun pulled out into disarray behind his head. Again, the desire to touch him stampeded through her, but she resisted and crept up the garden path and out of the gate. As she pushed it shut it squeaked. A soft melodic sound loud in the quiet street. She cringed, but he didn't move. She turned and ran lightly down the street a few meters then pulled on her boots.

A shadowy figure loomed up by the gate. Tya cringed back fearing her mother. Relief and angst swirled through her when she identified Stephanie and her child.

"What do you want, Stephanie?"

"I've come to tell you to stay away from my man. He's Stephen's father and we are going to be a family. "

Stephanie's words throttled through Tya demolishing the tiny sliver of hope she might have had. She gulped down the tears that threatened. There was no use crying. He would never have been hers anyway. *Then why was he asleep on her verandah. Why so determined to be with her if he already had other plans.*

She bit down on the words of protest that rose in her throat. "I think you're lying."

"How dare you call me a liar? We've just come from the doctor's clinic this morning getting the results. They confirmed Blake is the father. Here I'll show you." Stephanie shuffled in her bag.

Tya held up her hand. "Stop, I don't want to see."

"We're going to be a family so stay away. Get your hooks out of him."

"I suppose I should be pleased for you, but I'm not. It looks like you get what you wanted after all."

"I will. So, you stay away. If nothing else, you think of this little boy."

Tya looked down at the tiny baby bundled in the pram then up at Stephanie. "If you have nothing more to say I suggest you leave my property."

"Don't worry I'm going. But you keep in mind my warning or I'll spread your secrets from here to Timbuktu. Then see who wants you. Not Blake or any self-respecting man."

Tya slipped inside the gate and shut it firmly in Stephanie's face. She ran between the tomato bushes until she came to the shed. All was quiet. The tension buzzing through her eased to a vague tingle. She just had to water the seedlings tonight. None of the others were coming. It was peaceful in the garden. Tya took her time allowing the thoughts of Blake sleeping on her verandah to distract her. Maybe he had come to tell her he was the child's father and that he was going to reunite with Stephanie to make a happy family. Despite Stephanie's predictions she doubted it. He had been so adamant that whatever was between him and Stephanie was well and truly over. Obviously, Stephanie still feared her presence in Blake's life despite her revelations in the restaurant. This woman could be lying about her baby. Tya wasn't sure how she felt about the whole issue but in the end it wouldn't really concern her.

After watering the seedlings she made a lonely, melancholy walk back to the house. Dark clouds gathered on the horizon and flashes of lightening lit the distant hills. A storm brewed.

Tya dreaded facing Blake. He still sat in the chair, but he was wide awake and waiting for her. He didn't move from the chair as she climbed the steps.

"You snuck out and left me snoring here in the chair."

She smiled. "I did. You should have gone home."

"I don't want to. I came to tell you the child's not mine."

"What? Stephanie came to the garden tonight. She said the child was yours and you were getting back together."

"She's lying, Tya."

"She also said she would spread the information about my background to all your potential employees and business contacts if I didn't stay away."

"She already has."

"I can't do that to you, Blake. Go now before it gets any worse."

"I've warned her. Besides she has her own nasty secret now so she'll keep quiet."

"What."

"She'll lose her job and reputation if the real identity of her baby's father is revealed."

"It's not...the other man...Connor?"

"Nope."

He stood and took her into his arms before she could step back out of his reach. Once he touched her there was no withdrawing. She could not resist.

"Tya, my love, I care for you and the hurt to you if Stephanie tells stories, but it is all irrelevant to me what she says. Besides I'm not in law anymore. I'm running my father's company. For myself I don't give a damn. I don't need law and I don't need politics. All I need is you."

She looked up at him tears blurring her vision. "You might say that now, but what if a few years down the track you resent losing your career. What if we have a fight will you throw that at me? I've got nothing to lose, you have everything. What if I suddenly become addicted? What if you want to have children and I'm a lousy mother just like my own? Will you still love me then?"

"First and foremost, Tya, you are not going to be a lousy mother or become addicted to substances out of your control and most importantly I promise never to blame you for my own choices."

"But..."

His mouth smothered her words and caressed her lips until they vibrated to their own song. He scooped her into his arms. "We are going inside and I am going to ravish you until you can't think anymore and there will be no more protests because I will kiss you and love you until the protests die in your throat.

"Blake."

"After I have loved you thoroughly, I intend to introduce you to my family."

"Will they accept me, especially your father?"

"Do not worry, my darling, Tya. They will love you, just as much as me."

***

She dressed carefully in the plum colored dress she had been wearing the day they met. Blake had gone home early to change and he would be back at any moment to collect her. She struggled to spike her hair with trembling hands. While Blake had been with her she felt strong, but now alone, she fretted on this meeting. It would mean everything to Blake for this meeting to go well.

The car pulled up outside with a quiet grumble. She opened the door. Blake grinned. "Are you ready?"

She shook her head. "Yes...sort of, but I'm scared."

He pulled her into his embraced and kissed her gently on the mouth. "There is no reason to be scared. I'm right here."

"But what if they don't like me? I could never ask you to choose."

"I won't have to choose. Come."

He guided her to the car and helped her inside.

He slipped in beside her. He took her hand for a moment and squeezed. "It will be fine, Tya."

He held her around the waist as they walked out onto the terrace. Alice came forward. "Welcome, Tya." She hugged Tya then dropped a light kiss on her cheek.

"Thank you."

Rhiana burst out the doors. "Hello Tya. I knew that first day at the markets you two were meant for each other. The way my big brother kissed you I knew it was more than pretend.

"Sis, enough."

She giggled and clasped Tya's arm. "Come sit by me. Dad will be here in a minute."

Tya allowed herself to be guided away from Blake to the table. She slid into the chair and accepted the glass of apple juice Rhiana handed her. Tremors shuddered through her. The beautiful home overwhelmed her. It was a palace compared to her humble abode.

"I'll go and get Dad if you like, Alice."

"Good idea Blake

Tya waited in trepidation for the final test of acceptability. Tya already thought a great deal of Blake's father for him to even have her here, a drug addict's daughter in love with his son.

"So, Tya how's the new hoe working."

"It's fantastic. We have all the empty beds prepared for the winter crops. It's so much easier to use. Blake really shouldn't have though."

"Yes, he should have after what he did to your garden."

Tya laughed. "And he says he still loves me even though I tried to drown him."

"Huh he deserved it."

Tya liked Rhiana.

Prickles of fear rampaged through her body. Sweat beaded across her palms and she moved restively on her chair as Blake wheeled his father out onto the terrace.

When Blake beckoned she struggled to rise and step forward on shaky legs.

Muir Gifford smiled and held out his hands. "Welcome to the family Tya."

"Thank you for making me welcome, Mr. Gifford."

"How could I not welcome the woman who has mended my son's heart and taught him to trust in love again."

"Even if I'm unsuitable."

Blake frowned at her.

Muir Gifford smiled. "Pfff enough of this unsuitable business. You love him?"

She nodded.

"Can he trust you with his heart?"

She nodded.

"Then what is to be unsuitable. Now sit everyone, let's eat."

They talked about Tya's guerilla gardening ventures and how it helped those struggling with the rising cost of living.

"I would really love to do more. Community gardens in every neighborhood and in all the schools encouraging kids to garden so they are better equipped for the future."

"How many blocks do you garden on Tya?"

Tya smiled at Rhiana. "With the main one on Thistle Street we have five other blocks around the suburbs but they are looked mostly by the others. I just facilitate connections in the community and advise. Three are managed by members of the surrounding community. Nothing is sold from them it's all donated."

Rhiana reached out and touched Tya's arm. "That's wonderful Tya. You are such a caring person. More people should do it more me included."

Blake grinned. "What do you think Dad could we incorporate a community garden in some of our developments of low-cost housing projects? It might mean losing a house or two."

Muir frowned. "It could be done. Talk to William and Linley. We don't want to compromise profits."

Blake leaned toward his father. "It would be worth it to improve the environment and build community values. We can afford to make the sacrifice."

"It's up to you son. You're running the company now and I know you have always yearned to make the world a better place. I believe that's why you took up law."

Blake smiled. "It was Dad but it didn't turn out the way I expected." He turned to Tya. "Looks like we have a project."

Pleasure and gratitude raced through her. "That would fantastic Blake. We can work on it together."

"I'll help too." I'll use the Public Relations skills I'm learning at University.

Alice sat back in the chair beaming. "So, Blake no more law?"

He shook his head. "No I lost my passion for it after the Rochester Case. I still feel guilty that it was us that put him back on the street."

"And politics?"

"No. I spent most of my time in Hawaii rescuing turtles and helping preserve the habitat. It made me feel energetic, excited and positive. I think the gardening thing is going to make me feel the same. I am so aware of how lucky I've been being brought up in wealth and having made some of my own. I think it's time to give back."

Blakes father leaned back in the chair. "You're probably right Blake. I'm sure you will manage it appropriately with Tya to advise you."

"Thanks Dad."

After their farewells they drove in silence toward her home. Tya lay back in the encompassing leather chair. A soft sigh of contentment whispered out on her breath. She looked at Blake.

He met her gaze and his grin widened. "So not so bad, my love?"

She shook her head. "Not bad at all. Your family is so kind, Alice is lovely, your father such a gentleman and Rhiana wants to treat me like a sister."

"Well, you will be soon."

"You have no doubts, Blake."

"Absolutely none."

They climbed out of the car and ambled up the over-grown garden path arms entwined. On the top step Blake paused and looked down at her. His breath caressed her cheeks as his hands strayed up and down her back. He lowered his head.

Every nerve ending tingled with anticipation rushed His body heat warmed her.

The hair on her arms lifted, prickling her skins. Her pussy dampened. She ran her arms up over his, rising onto her toes until their lips met, gentle, exploring, caressing. Tya stepped closer and pressed her body to his.

He released her lips and kissed her eyelids, cheeks and down her neck into her cleavage.

Her legs trembled and her breath jagged in her chest. Exquisite sensation flowed through her, warm, moist and liquid leaving a trail of sparks tingling over her body.

"Open the door, my love, I want to love you."

She eased her hips away from his and fumbled in her bag for the keys. The contents rattled with the tremors of her hand.

"Shall I help you," Blake asked easing his hand in beside hers. He entwined his fingers with hers rubbing his thumb across her palm.

She gasped.

Then together their hands closed over the elusive keys.

Blake didn't release her hand as she went to withdraw it. He held it and raised it to his lips. He placed three feather soft kisses on the back of her hand even as he gazed into her eyes.

She stood entranced and didn't resist when he eased the keys from her grip and opened the door. He turned to her and kissed her lips again. "My darling, come inside so I can love you," he murmured against her mouth. He encircled her waist and eased her forward.

They didn't even register the scream of sirens until the pitch was so close it was unbearable and finally shattered their sensuous love bubble. The red and white lights searing through the soft dusky gloom.

"What the heck," Blake muttered as he peered back through the front door.

Two uniformed officers thudded up the garden path. Blake gently stood Tya down and turned to face their visitors.

"Officers?"

"Are you, Tya Morley?'

Tya nodded.

"You need to come immediately. Your mother's in a bad way. She appears to have given birth and it doesn't look good. They're putting her in an ambulance two streets away. She's asking for you."

"Take her to hospital, it's not my problem." Even as she said it a wrench of guilt sliced through her.

Tya looked up at Blake.

"Go, Tya, she's your mother, she needs you, if even to say goodbye. Come-on, we'll go together." Blake tucked his arm around her shoulders and guided her out into the street and into the police car. He climbed in beside her.

Tya clutched his hand.

"Thank you for coming."

He squeezed her hand. "I wouldn't not come, my love."

The multiple sets of emergency lights cast a moving kaleidoscope around the street filled with deepening shadows and highlighting open spaces. Her mother already lay on the stretcher when Tya ran to her side. There was blood everywhere.

"The baby," she asked the paramedics.

One shook her head.

The other said. "We couldn't find the infant. It has to be close by. She can't have walked far in her state."

Tya leaned over her mother. She was barely conscious. "Mum, I'm here. Where's the baby?"

Her mum waved her hands about, her eyes barely open. "I can't remember, it just came. Just like that."

"Concentrate. We need to find the baby or it will die."

Her mum cackled. "Don't matter, not much good for anything, just like me."

Tya grabbed her bony shoulders and shook her roughly barely holding the fiery anger that consumed her in check. "Mum, you have to remember."

"Can't. Just came out."

"Mum tell me where the child is."

"I don't remember. It just came out. I don't remember where the little bastard is."

The paramedic tried to treat her, but she flailed her arms at him pushing him out the way.

"The baby will die. Please if you care at all, tell me."

Suddenly rain poured down.

Her mum cackled. "I even stayed clean for it as well but now its gone."

"Mum..."

"A cabbage patch kid that's what it is, a cabbage patch kid."

Blake leaned forward his expression grim. "Do you know what she means?"

Tya shook her head then stopped and pushed to her feet. Urgency whipped at her even as panic caught in her throat. A sudden thought stabbed at her. "The garden. The baby's got to be in the garden."

"Mum, is it in the garden?"

Her mum moaned her eyes rolling back in her head as she lost consciousness.

"We have to get her to hospital."

"Take her away she's no use anyway." Tya flung away from the trolley as it was slid into the ambulance and ran in the direction of the garden.

"Wait, Tya," Blake yelled.

She struggled to breathe against the sobs choking her chest. Damn her mother. The poor child. She didn't believe her mother for a moment that she was clean.

Lightning flashed overhead and huge drops of rain splattered on her head. The pavement jarred her feet in her light sandals, tears and rain blended together.

With a slapping swipe she brushed the blinding liquid off her face. With wet fingers Tya fumbled with the latch her haste hampering her dexterity.

A car pulled in behind her. She glanced over her shoulder. It was a female constable and Blake. The rain poured down drenching all three of them to the skin. The police constable handed her a large torch, and they moved in unison through the rows of plants. She ignored the wet leaves slapping at her and refused to be daunted by the thunder and lightning crashing around her. Mud slid into her sandals and Tya scrunched her toes to keep her footing. Her hair plastered to her skull and she wiped the raindrops off her eyelids.

Got to find it. Got to find it. Thoughts skittered around and around in her head. She wiped her face and peered under the pumpkin bushes. There were no cabbages because it was the wrong season.

"Tya, keep looking. More officers are coming."

"Thanks, Blake."

She moved through the pumpkin patch and onto the wide bed filled with zucchini plants. They were so vigorous she had to push her way through the plants. Her heart battered an uneven rhythm behind her breast. She clenched her fists the urge to scream burned in her throat. Bush after bush revealed nothing. Tya paused to listen but heard only the sound of the rain sloshing on the wet ground and periodic rumbles of thunder moving slowly towards the hills. She headed for the rows of tomatoes and for a fleeting moment silence engulfed her as the rain petered out to a few large drops.

A plaintive sound teased her, stopped and came again. It sounded like a kitten.

Tya gulped and turned her head back and forth squashing her panic down to listen more closely.

The cry came again. One that could only be a baby.

Shaking with sheer desperation Tya tore foliage aside as she hunted through the plants row after row. The sound was more infrequent, softer, and weaker. She moved faster through the rows. The clouds slid away, and the moon bathed the garden with silver light. Something moved, just a slightest of movement by the compost frame. A muted blotch of white. Tya gulped back sobs. "Blake, Blake I've found the baby." Her voice cracked as she leapt at the compost heap.

She clutched the wooden planks holding herself upright. Relief, fear and anguish twisted in her stomach. Her stomach lurched.

The naked baby lay covered in blood, the cord still attached to the navel. There was blood everywhere.

She took off her cardigan and scooped the baby up from the ground.

The little girl mewed weakly. The tiny hands clenched into fists and flailed the air.

An unexpected explosion of warmth and love clutched her heart as she hugged the baby to her breasts. It was wet and cold.

The rosebud mouth puckered up and made sucking noises. The baby cried again.

Something burst in Tya's chest swamping her underlying fear she was not maternal. In that moment Tya knew she would give her life for this child. She cuddled the baby to her rocking it from side to side murmuring loving words. Tears poured down her face. This was her sister. Left here to die in the mud. The rain started again. Huge drops plopping onto her head.

She looked up.

Blake approached his torch flashing. "Thank goodness you've found it."

"She's so tiny, cold and barely moving." Her words were croaked and broken. Her chest clenched tight again and again. Desperation flooded through her. She couldn't let her baby sister die. She was covered in birthing mess and her cord hung loose on her abdomen. Tya's heart nearly burst with love. This poor little being was her sibling. The child reached out and latched onto Tya's finger and clung to it with desperation.

Blake wrapped his arm around her shoulders and guided her though the garden and into the police car. The constable radioed ahead that they were coming in with a newborn premature infant. The police car had its lights flashing and siren screaming and in no time at all they were pulling into the Women's and Children's Hospital.

The bright lights eased Tya's panic. The baby was no longer making any effort to move. She just laid there her little mouth open, eyes closed and fists clenched.

Blake wrapped his arms around Tya as the nurses hurried away with the child.

"She would have died if we hadn't found her. Damn my mother, all the way to hell."

"She probably didn't mean to hurt the baby deliberately. She claimed she stayed clean for the baby."

Tya huddled closer to his hard chest. "Too little too late Blake. If she really cared she would have done something about her addiction even before she had me. I know she's had a hard life, but most of it was her own making. I am going to fight for custody of the child if she lives. I will not let my mother damage another child like she has me and the boys. I can give her a decent upbringing."

"We can, Tya. We can do it together."

"Blake, that child is not your responsibility. This is even more reason for us not to get together. You made it clear before you don't want to be raising some unknown man's child. This is not only an unknown man's; it's a whore's child. She's already addicted to heroin. Hear her screaming. She might have brain damage. It's not fair to tie you down to that. Her voice broke and tears welled up in her eyes.

"Shhh. I only meant I didn't want another man's child foisted on me in secret. To be lied to. This baby is different. I'd be choosing to bring it up."

"I can't let you, Blake."

"Who's going to stop me? You and what army?" He hugged her close."

They sat together for almost an hour before the nurse came and said they could go in. They had to gown up in blue gowns and wear masks. The little baby lay in a humid crib on an opti flow and wires stuck to her body. She screamed and writhed, flailing the air with her tiny fists. Tear dribble formed in her eyes that were squeezed shut with the effort of crying and against the pain.

"She's coming off the drugs. It could be a few days before we see an improvement."

Tya reached out and touched the glass. "She's so small."

The nurse gave her a stern look. "She is very underweight and about three weeks prem. None of that helps her start in life, in addition to her addiction to heroin. I get so angry at mothers who do this to their child."

Tya pressed both hands against the glass. "So, do I. My mother did it to me and now she has done it to my little sister and there was nothing I could do to stop her."

She turned when someone placed their hand on her shoulder.

"Ms Morley can you come with me. Your mother is in a bad way and she's asking for you."

Tya didn't know how she felt. She was angry at her mother, and resentful but tiny threads of love remained tugging at her heart.

Tya sighed. "Yes, I'll come."

She followed the doctor down the corridor aware of Blake striding right behind her.

She entered the room. Her mother lay in the bed. She was pale and haggard. Machines peeped and clattered.

Her mother reached out to her. "Tya thank you for coming."

Tya walked over to the bed but couldn't quite bring herself to take her mother's hands.

Her mother let them fall to the bed. "Tya I'm sorry. I'm a rotten mother. I should never have had children."

"But you did Mum and you never changed. Never made an effort to help us or yourself."

Tears poured down her mother's face. "I tried but I couldn't. I'm sorry for what I did to you and your brothers. And that little mite in there I stopped using after you yelled at me." She pointed to the corner of the room. "I tried but it wasn't enough I know."

"She might die yet Mum."

"I know Tya, I know and it's all my fault."

"It is Mum."

"I'm sorry. The doctors have told me I'm in a bad way. They haven't been able to stop the bleeding. I'm afraid Tya. I'm going to die."

Tya looked across at the doctor. He nodded.

Blake stepped up behind her and placed his hand on her shoulder.

"Mum I'm sorry you're going to die."

"Tya please forgive me for all the bad I've done. Please."

Tya stared down at this dying woman who gave birth to her. She had never been a mother to her. Resentment swelled up but as she stared down at her tendrils of sympathy weaved through her.

"Please Tya love, please forgive me?"

Tya reached out and placed her hand on her mother's. "I forgive you Mum."

Her mother clasped her hand. "Thank you, Tya. Now I can die in peace."

Tya pulled her hand away. "What about the baby Mum? What are you going to do about that poor little baby? She'll have no mother or father, no home, nothing."

Tya's mother sobbed then took a deep breath. "She'll have you, Tya."

"But Mum she needs a mother."

"You'll be a better Mum to her than I could ever be, ever was. I leave her to you Tya."

Tya turned to Blake. "Can she do this. Just leave her child to me."

Blake nodded. "She can but it needs to be in writing. Does she have a will?"

Evalina Morley shook her head. "Never seen the need ain't thought I'd be dying so soon."

Blake stepped back. "Then she needs one. He turned and left the room already tapping on his phone.

Confused, Tya sank into the chair by the bed her hands clasped in her lap. Her mother lay back on the pillow and closed her eyes. She seemed to be muttering something. Tya leaned forward and heard the whispered words of the Lord's prayer.

She pulled away. The door whispered open and shut behind her. Blake appeared behind her. He handed her a piece of paper. The heading was last will and testament of Evalina Morley of no fixed address.

"She needs to read and sign it with a couple of witnesses."

Tya read the document. It was simple.

She touched her mother's shoulder. She opened her eyes.

"Mum you need to read this and sign it so I can have the baby."

The doctor came forward and with the help of the nurse gently lifted Tya's mother into a semi sitting position.

Tya gave her the document.

She began to read. "No." She shook her head. "This is not right."

Blake stepped forward. "Mrs. Morley what do you want it to say?"

Tya's mother looked up at Blake. "Oh, you're that posh bloke from the house."

Blake nodded. "Yes I am."

"Well, if you are so posh you need to re-write this. It's not just the baby I'm leaving her. I want to leave everything I own to Tya. Now go fix it."

"But Mum you don't have anything to leave."

Her mother looked at her. "You know nothing Tya. Now shut up and let your posh fella fix it."

Blake had already left the room.

Her mother drifted off into semi consciousness. Tya shivered as she waited for Blake to return.

Less than ten minutes later Blake pushed into the room. He was accompanied by a tall thin man with a shaved head, a goatee and a large diamond earing in his left ear.

Blake held the new document out to Tya. This time it was printed on the letter head of Tydeman, Williams and Grosvenor, Solicitors.

Tya handed it to her mother.

"She has to be in her right mind for it to be legal. What about drugs in her system?"

"I haven't used for the last three weeks trying for the baby. She peered at the document. "That's more like it.

All my estate, goods and chattels to Tya Morley and Testamentary Guardianship of baby Morley, born this day to Tya Morley. Give us a pen."

The doctor provided the pen and the nurse slid the over way across the bed.

Her mother was gasping for breath, sweat beading on her face. She took the pen. Tya flattened the papers on the over way. "Are you sure about this Mum?"

"Yes, I'm sure. It'll be the only good thing I've ever done for you and that little one."

Her hand shook as she scratched her signature at the appropriate spot. She handed the pen to the doctor. "Your turn matey, and hurry up before I cark it on ya."

The doctor added his signature and name then pushed the document across to the nurse. She took the pen and added her credentials and signature to each page.

"Good, it's done. *Now* I can die in peace."

Emotion rushed through Tya. No matter how she felt about her Mum the thought of her actually dying cut through her. They had never had much of a relationship even when she was little and Tya mourned that loss and what would now never be."

She sat with her mother through the night and in the early hours of the next day Evalina Morley took her last breath.

As they covered her face with a sheet Tya left the room.

Blake embraced her as she emerged. "Are you okay."

Tya nodded. "I'm okay. Mum and I weren't ever close. It's sad she died so young but she had a miserable life. I'll organize a private cremation then it will be over. There is no need for a memorial service and I don't want one."

None of her brothers would acknowledge their mother's passing.

It was several days after her mother died before Tya could even hold the baby. But when she eventually could the emotion washed over her again in a tidal wave of pain, love and awe. The nurse gave her a bottle and she fed her sister.

Blake stood behind her watching her interact with the baby. He knew then and there that she did have maternal instincts contrary to what she claimed. She was a natural. The baby soon dozed off in the safe embrace of her sister.

"You've chosen a name then?" the nurse asked.

Tya looked first at the nurse then at Blake. "The child is not mine, she's my sister, but my mother abandoned her. Do I have the right to name her?"

Blake grinned. "Your mother left her to you and I don't think the family court will disapprove your guardianship and definitely won't change the name you choose."

The nurse smiled. "At least give her a temporary name it's nicer to call her by name instead of Baby Morley."

She looked up again at Blake. He smiled. "You chose. She is your sister."

"I think I'll call her Caitlin."

CHAPTER 10

T ya spent every minute with Caitlin at the hospital that her other commitments allowed and most evenings Blake came with her.

"Come on hand her over. I want a hold."

Tya smiled and placed Caitlin in Blake's arms. She watched as he gave his finger into her grasp. He leaned in and lightly placed a kiss on the child's forehead. He seemed so comfortable with his tiny bundle. Love for him exploded inside before scattering right through her. Her mind still struggled with the knowledge that this man, handsome, rich, smart, funny and loving, loved her and seemed to love this tiny fragile baby of a drug addicted prostitute.

She knew her guardianship was temporary until approved by the Family Court and while she doubted her brothers would apply for custody she worried about the future. Blake assured her there was very little chance she would lose Caitlin.

***

The days passed quickly as Tya soaked up the love that surrounded her. In between visiting the hospital and working her business, Tya worked in the garden. Endeva was supportive of her move to have the baby but still wasn't convinced Blake was good for her. Blake worked long hours but tried to come and help her in the garden most nights.

It was cooler tonight so Tya decided to take Blake to the other gardens she had. Four altogether plus Thistle Street. When he arrived, she was waiting for him just outside the gate Caitlin blissfully snoring in her holder.

She waved to him and crossed the road as he got out of the Land Cruiser and opened the back door.

"Finished early tonight." He dived in for a quick kiss as he took Caitlin.

"Yes, with the cooler weather there is less watering to do, but I thought you should see the other gardens we have. Just so you know what you're getting into."

Blake chuckled as he backed out of the car. "I don't care what I'm into as long as it includes you." He drew her into his embrace and proceeded to kiss her very thoroughly. As he released her mouth he said, "I could take you home right now and ravish you instead."

Tya grinned. "Caitlin might have an objection to that she's due for a bottle shortly."

Blake grinned. "Can I have a raincheck?"

Tya stood on tip toes and fleetingly kissed his mouth that was turned down in a pretend pout. "Of course you can."

As they settled in the car Tya turned to him. "You don't mind having a raincheck. You don't resent the limitations Caitlin has brought."

He turned the ignition then squeezed her hand. "Not at all Tya now where are these gardens?"

She gave him the address then directed him.

There were three people at the garden.

"Hi guys."

They all looked toward her. "Hiya Tya."

Clara stepped forward. She reached out and touched Tya's arm gently. "Sorry for your loss Tya."

Tya smiled. "Thank you, Clara. It was a shock but I wasn't that close to my mother."

Clara looked up at Blake then down at the baby. "So, this is your fella and the poor little tyke."

"Tya grinned. "Yes, this is Blake and my baby sister Caitlin. We've just stopped by so Blake can see the gardens."

Clara smiled. "The crops are doing well. We've just distributed four boxes of tomatoes and two of corn to the food bank on Hanson Road and we have just transplanted the cabbages out as its almost the end of February.

"Great they'll do well as it cools down."

Caitlin whimpered.

Tya looked across at Blake. "We will have to go someone is going to be demanding food shortly."

"Come back soon Tya and spend some time."

"I will."

They climbed back in the car and the ride to the next garden Caitlin drifted back to sleep. As they pulled up Tya saw it. A real estate for sale sign planted in the middle of the block with a large red Sold sticker across it. Tya could see people moving amongst the plants.

"What the heck. It can't be sold. The others haven't said anything. I was here just two weeks ago."

Blake brought the car to a stop. "Go see what's going on I'll stay here and mind Caitlin. Come back and tell me what goes."

Tya ran across the road and into the garden.

Sarah ran toward her. "Tya thank goodness you're here. We didn't even know the block was up for sale and then the sold sign went up today. The land agent has told us we have one month to get off the block."

"Do you know who bought it?

"The land agent wouldn't tell us."

"Okay don't worry. I'll check it out. Just don't plant any more seedlings out."

She ran back to Blake. She could hear Cailtin crying. She climbed into the car.

"Tya?"

Tears filled her eyes. "The block has been sold and we've been kicked out."

"Oh Tya."

"Well, it's not ours so it was bound to happen eventually. Let's go home Blake. Caitlin needs her bottle."

"I can check it out, Tya."

"It might be too late for that Blake."

"Maybe but I think we should purchase the other block."

"Really, you would do that for me.... For the battlers who need the vegies?"

"Of course. I have lots of ideas we can discuss later."

Caitlin was beginning to scream as they pulled into her driveway. They hurried inside and Blake made her bottle while Tya changed her diaper.

Blake was already settled in the scruffy armchair with the bottle and a chuck rag. Tya smiled and passed the wriggling baby to Blake. As soon as the nipple touched her mouth she fell silent except for suckling slurps.

When Caitlin was settled in her cradle Blake scooped Tya up and carried her to the bedroom.

He stood down before him and with teasing slowness he undressed her. Slipping the straps of her sundress leisurely over her shoulders one at a time, kissing her skin as the material passed over it.

She ran her fingers through his hair releasing his blond locks from the ties. It tumbled untidily onto his shoulders.

He lifted his head and brushed his mouth over hers.

Her lips tingled. A sigh of desire meandered through her. She embraced the teasing warmth.

Blake's hands gently pushed the shirred bodice of her dress down exposing her breasts. With an almost idle movement of his thumbs he circled her nipples enticing them erect before brushing over the tips igniting a fiery tingle where skin touched skin.

Tya slipped her arms free of her straps and reached up to undo the buttons of his shirt.

He lifted his head again and captured her mouth with his. His lips melded with hers, caressing and exploring before he released her mouth with a lingering suck on her bottom lip.

His shirt fell away as she pushed it off his shoulders. She stroked his hard contours of his chest and abdomen with the softness of her fingertips.

He inhaled deeply then exhaled a long slow sigh his warm breath wafting over her bare skin.

She leaned in and placed butterfly light kisses across the hard muscles.

His flesh shivered and twitched. A soft moan vibrated through his chest. "Oh Tya I need you so much."

Her fingers fumbled with the belt of his shorts.

He pushed her dress down over her hips and it floated to the floor.

Moments later his shorts shushed to the floor.

Tya ran her hands over the front of his trunks, teasingly squeezing the hardness of his erection.

He moaned and eased his crotch closer into her hands.

She cupped his balls massaging lightly before tugging the waistband over his hips and releasing his hard hot shaft from its confines. Stroked the length of his cock reveling in the hot silky hardness. A shudder rippled along his flesh under the movement of her hand as she circled the satiny smoothness of his head.

He groaned. "God Tya what you do to me. Your touch is more than a man can bear." He eased her backward until her thighs touched the edge of the bed.

She allowed herself to tumble backwards and settle on the bed.

He gripped her hips and slid her panties off slowly sensually all the way down her legs. As they fell to the floor he kissed her toes then ankles moving with tormenting slowness up her legs.

She whimpered and squirmed. "I want you Blake."

He glanced at her and grinned. "I know. And you will have me...soon." He continued to kiss and nuzzle up her legs moving closer as he reached her inner thighs. With the slightest pressure he parted her legs and trailed kisses right up to her mound. With his hands under her buttocks he lifted her slightly then dipped his face into her hot wetness.

Tya stifled a scream of ecstasy as his tongue delved into her pussy exploring her flesh, tangling his tongue around her clit. She clenched the bed sheets arched her back and tipped her head back as a tsunami of fiery rapture engulfed her. She bit down on her cries. Tremors surged through her.

Then his fingers slipped inside her thrusting and stroking.

She writhed surrendering to the height of bliss as her orgasm crashed through her. She panted and trembled tiny frissons pulsed through her as she collapsed into the mattress.

She opened her eyes.

Blake lifted his head and stilled his fingers for a moment. He waited watching her a satisfied smile quirky his mouth up.

"Blake?"

He moved his fingers softly inside her.

She gasped.

He ran his thumb over her clit with whisper gentleness.

Her pussy throbbed. She inhaled. And lifted her hips and clenched her muscles to enclose his fingers.

"Again, my love?"

She nodded already feeling the sensations gathering in her nether regions.

He continued to stroke and penetrate her with his fingers. He watched her closely.

She sighed and whimpered softly. Her pussy pulsed as he next orgasm built.

He brushed her clit.

She bit down on her cries and clenched his fingers with her inner muscles.

Blake moved close his fingers still caressing her. He moved over her sensually withdrawing his fingers.

She barely registered their absence as his cock dipped into her pussy, just the head then withdrew.

"God Blake, take me."

Again his cock slipped into her pussy just an inch or two before withdrawing.

Tya reached up and grabbed his shoulders digging her nails into his flesh. "Blake please for Gods sake." She felt his chuckle. She watched him.

He watched her. Again he penetrated her moistness and withdrew not right out but just leaving the tip of his cock inside.

Her whole body pulsed and quivered. Her orgasm was on the brink of exploding. The pleasure, the bliss hovered goading her body. Wave after wave of warm thrills rippled through her.

Again he thrust into her and withdrew almost all the way.

"Oh God. I can't stand it."

"Do you want it Tya. All of it. Are you ready."

"Oh Blake take me."

"Like this my love." He thrust hard and deep again and again.

She gasped. Sensation pounded through her wave after wave with each thrust of his cock. She bit her lip against her screams. Her body shuddered, she gasped for air, stars crackled and blinked around her head. Her pussy clenched again and again.

Blake continued to thrust. Hard, fast and deep.

Tya pulled her muscles around his cock but couldn't hold it as she tumbled, throbbing and vibrating in ecstasy. She clawed his shoulders and thrust up to meet him. She struggled to breathe flying on the wings of her pleasure.

Above her Blake groaned and thrust deep before he stilled.

They collapsed in a sweaty sated heap. The only sound in the room was their gasping struggles for breath.

Blake claimed her mouth in a hard demanding kiss before sliding out of her and off her. He cuddled close nuzzling her neck.

Tya trembled and shuddered with aftershocks.

Blake gently caressed her mound.

Tya moaned as his touch soothed her throbbing flesh.

He kissed her lightly then stared into her eyes. She stared back. Nothing needed to be said.

Blake rose early. He leaned in and kissed her. "Sleep Tya until Caitlin wakes again. I'm going to work. Don't worry about the block I'll check it out and see what I can do."

Tya snuggled down. "Thank you, Blake."

She woke to Caitlin's cries two hours later. It was already getting hot outside. She needed to get to the garden and help water. It didn't take long and then they retreated to the air conditioner.

The sun had just set and the whole garden glowed gold and pink in the dusk light. Tya stopped past the fountain and stood staring into the water.

"Tya."

She turned to face Blake. He went down on one knee. She shivered, overwhelmed at the gesture and so uncertain about him doing it.

"Tya my love will you do me the honor of becoming my wife? I love you, admire and respect you. I want to share my life with you forever."

Tears welled up in her eyes. To sight of him kneeling so humbly there on the warm pavers a small proposal ring held up so it glinted in the fading light.

She trembled. Could she do this? Could it possibly last a lifetime?

She stepped forward.

"Blake, you know my background. You know the risks and yet you still ask."

He nodded. "Of course, because I love you."

She stepped closer and took his hands in hers. He rose to his feet. He looked deeply into her eyes. "Say yes, Tya. Please."

He pulled her against his chest and held her in a gentle embrace. "Just say yes, Tya," he whispered against her hair.

"But I'm sacred, Blake. Scared of ruining your life, of destroying what we have right now."

He pulled her closer. "Well, I'm not scared, Tya. I'm sure and I'm brave enough for both of us Trust me Tya. I have enough strength for both of us."

"Oh Blake, how can you be so sure."

"There are no guarantees, Tya, but our love is strong, I am strong and we will work it out together. I will never let you down. Do you understand from this moment I am your rock, your port in a storm? I will always be here for you to lean on."

"That sounds so one sided."

He put her from him so he could see her face. "It is your love that makes me strong so it's not one sided at all. Please say yes. Be mine forever."

Tya heart fluttered with joy and love infused with fear. She wanted to love this man, marry him and raise a family. Since Caitlin's arrival she had discovered she did indeed have maternal instincts. Something exploded inside and as it faded a warm contented feeling singing in her veins, she pushed the doubts aside. "Yes, I'll marry you."

He hugged her to him and leaned down to take command of her mouth. Softy at first then with passionate zeal he plundered the soft flesh, branding her his forever. He caressed her lips and nibbled at them before he released her. He picked up her hand and slipped the ring on her finger.

"We will pick out the real one together. I wasn't sure what you would like and as you actually make jewelery, I thought I better consult."

Tya giggled. "Getting the ring right is going to be the least of your worries in the coming years. You know that don't you?"

Blake chuckled. "Probably, but I don't care."

They sat on the chair and listened to the water trickle down the fountain. Tya relaxed in the warmth of his embrace and sought his mouth again and again reveling in the taste and feel of him.

***

Together they walked home in the early evening light. This time there was no rush, no urgency to their lovemaking.

They had all their lives to express themselves and satisfy the burning fire of need that tortured both of them.

With the only light the bedside lamp on low Blake touched her face with gentle stroked outline each curve and feature with the tips of his fingers. Tya stood still under his exploration. As he slid his fingers into the curve of her neck he leaned in and lightly kissed her face. First her lips than her eyes, cheeks and ears.

Sensation sizzled inside but Tya remained motionless, absorbing the gentle touches of love. He slid his fingers around the neckline of her top then back up to slide the straps over her shoulders and down he arms. The top slipped exposing the upper swell of her breasts. Blake leaned in and kissed them in turn than trailed kisses up her cleavage, neck and back to claim he mouth.

Tya sucked in air to fill her starving lungs. Her knees softened and she clenched her thighs together as if she could capture the rioting sensation dancing between them. But it wouldn't be contained and with exploding tendrils the desire spread until her whole lower body glowed with need.

Blake brought his fingers back to her top sliding it sensuously over her breasts and down to her hips. Her nipples were taut and erect deep rose pink nubs in the dark circle of her areola. Blake ravished them with his look first.

Tya's flesh swelled and warmed in anticipation of his touch.

He lowered his head and with excruciating gentleness he took one nipple in his mouth and swirled his tongue around the hard little nub.

Tya gasped and then moaned as sensation raced through her. Her heart thudded now in an erratic rhythm. The ache in her pussy weighed heavy and she relaxed her muscles into the pleasurable sensation. She felt the dampness pooling between her legs.

Then Blake nibbled on her other nipple.

She gasped in air as he sucked, softly then harder. A moan torn from her mouth.

"I love you."

"Mmm I love you too," he murmured against her skin as he cupped her breast with one hand and suckled intensely.

He lifted his head away and stared down into her eyes. "I told you I would do it properly one day."

"Mmmmm." Tya was unable to form a cohesive sentence in response.

Blake chuckled. "And I haven't finished yet."

With a tug he loosened her shorts and with careful precision slipped his hand inside her waistband and pushed. The shorts slid down over her hips and thighs and floated to the floor.

Tya kicked free of them without losing her equilibrium by holding onto Blake. She was naked now except for her lacy blue knickers.

Blake slipped his hand inside the lace covering and squeezed her buttocks as he pulled her closer. He trailed his fingers between her cheeks and down between her legs feeling his way ever so gently to her opening. He caressed the dampened flesh.

Tya gasped and wriggled as the sensation flared into a tornado of desire.

She clenched her legs cradling his hand with her inner flesh.

With a small tug he took his hand away and flicked her knickers over her bum and down her thighs.

Tya was craving flesh against flesh so she responded to his making her naked by lifting his t shirt up to exposure the sculptured muscular expanse of his chest. He cooperated by lifting his arms as she tugged the shirt upwards. With delicate strokes she traced the outline of his flesh with her fingertips. The hard bone and firm resistance of his muscles was sexy. She ran her fingers over his pecs and circled his nipples in smaller and smaller dizzying circles.

He watched her. His flesh hardened and his nipples became erect.

She lowered her head and sucked hard eliciting a moan of pleasure and encouragement rumbling through his chest. In a sensuous slide she moved her hands over his skin until they reached the waistband of his shorts where she inserted her fingers under the elastic and pushed coaxing the material over his hips and making sure she took his trunks with them.

Blake's erection jumped out hard and hot.

Tya enclosed the hard throbbing flesh with her hand and slid up and down the length in a rhythmic stroking.

Blake groaned again and pushed his cock toward her.

She moved away ever so slightly and looked down. His hard flesh caressed her abdomen and now she reached down and cupped his balls carefully rolling them around in the scrotum. Blake groaned loudly. Tya looked up at him. He had his head thrown back and his eyes closed. She stroked some more then moved back to his cock. She stroked the length using the moisture of pre cum to smooth her actions.

Blake trembled. "God Tya, I need you right now."

She stepped back and pulled him with her and they tumbled into a seething sexual heap. Blake reached for her and rolled her onto her back. She went obediently and parted her legs. Blake slid his hand into her fiery flesh and dipped into her fluids to ease his path into her pussy. He slid a couple of fingers inside and Tya cried out as bolts of sensation crackled through her abdomen and exited through her head. Her hips jerked against his invasion and he wriggled his fingers stroking the muscular walls of her pussy. Light exploded behind her eyes, sensation rushed dancing and twirling through her as the ache in her pussy imploded, concentrated inside then exploded taking reality with it on a rollercoaster ride through her body. Her legs jerked, her hips lifted and her toes curled.

"Oh oh oh, Mmm."

Her words were cut off by Blake claiming her mouth in a hard demanding kiss. She wrapped her arms around his neck and pulled him closer even as his fingers moved rhythmically inside her.

"Are you ready for the main course?" Blake whispered in her ear.

"Oh yes," she whispered back.

With sensuous slowness he withdrew his fingers from her pussy but not far just enough to seek out the nub of flesh that was the center of her pleasure.

He lubricated the layers of flesh with her own juices and tucked his fingers around her clitoris and stroked up and down the tiny length.

Tya squirmed with sweet sweet pleasure at first just in her clit but them it spread in a sizzling fan through her lips and into her pussy. Her body throbbed with waves after wave of pleasure. Conscious of it building she reached between them and clasped his cock gently urging him closer to her entrance.

Blake kissed her mouth cheeks and eyelids then buried his face in the nape of her neck to muffle his moans as she stroked his cock, some soft some hard.

He slid across and covered her with his body.

She settled back her legs apart. She felt the hardness of his cock touching her flesh. And she guided him to her entrance. The air in her lungs launched out of her throat leaving her gasping as he slid into her filling her and triggering an avalanche of sensation. She trembled. He thrust and she lifted her hips to meet each of his downward strokes.

He watched her intently.

She stared back at him not afraid to let him see her passion. She pressed her legs against his hips as the sensation built layer on layer as he thrust hard and deep bringing her onto the cusp of the storm. Sensation billowed through her body until she could barely take a breath. Still he thrust. Everything centered on where their flesh joined and all Tya could feel was the throb and lurch of his cock as it was buried in her again and again. The sweetness of sexual arousal swamped her, tingling through every nerve prompted by the hardness of his cock and the abrasion of his thrusts. She moaned and pushed up to meet him the sensation burst and roared through her body leaving her flesh fiery and trembling in its wake.

He penetrated hard and groaned, pausing for a moment to revel in the undulating throbs of pleasure that rippled the length of his cock.

Tya collapsed beneath him swimming in a boneless satiation that defied description. Her muscles ached with effort but at the same time relaxed with completion. She gasped in breaths.

The tension seeped out of Blake and he sagged on top of her. He rested his face on her breasts, struggling to increase his intake of air.

Tya stroked his head gently with undirected movements of her floppy hands.

He made no attempt to withdraw his cock and they lay joined for quite a while the only sound was their uneven breathing and the hum of traffic in the distance.

Blake groaned as he levered himself off Tya and rolled onto the bed beside her. "And that we shall have every day from now on," he murmured.

Tya giggled.

He turned on his side and embraced her tightly.

"Forever."

CHAPTER 11

Tya looked up from where she was kneeling in the dark earth planting cabbage seedlings. Endeva sat in the chair gently rocking with Caitlin cuddled on her lap. Her little fists waved in the air as Endeva chatted to her with gentle baby talk. Her heart swelled with love for the child and the woman holding her. Cailtin would have lots of adults to love her and guide her through her life. She would have a good life.

Tya turned back to her work loving the feel of the damp earth cradling the crisp green seedlings.

At the sound of approaching footsteps she looked back up. Blake appeared through the two tomato beds.

He was dressed in a suit. Even as she admired his sexy look she knew she preferred him in work shorts and tee.

She rose and brushed the dirt from her hands and climbed out of the garden bed.

"I have something to show you Tya do you have time to come with me?"

She looked down at herself and grinned. "I'm a little under dressed don't you think?"

He grinned back and raised his eyebrows. "If I had any choice I'd say you're over dressed and I should do something about it."

The heat flooded through her body a gently pulsing tension building in her nether regions. She placed her hands on her hips and lifted her chin slightly. "Really Mr. Gifford."

"Yes really, but I have something more pressing. Can you come?"

Tya glanced at Endeva. The older woman nodded. "Miss Caitlin and I will be fine until you come back. We have a bottle and diapers."

"Are you sure?"

"Endeva you can come too if you would like?"

Endeva shook her head. "

The boys will be here soon and someone has to supervise them or those rows of cabbages with have more kinks than a dog's hind leg."

"Thanks, Endeva. We won't be long."

Tya walked over and washed her hands under the tap. She dried them on her shorts.

Blake reached out and took her hand tugging her toward the gate.

"What has got you so excited Blake?"

"It's a surprise."

As he got in the car Blake shed his jacket and tie, undid his cuffs and rolled his sleeves up. "That's better. He leaned over and cupped the side of her face and took possession of her mouth. She melted and responded to his demanding exploration. He dipped his tongue in her mouth and she tangled her tongue around his. They were both breathless when they finally parted. Blake turned forward and started the car. "Almost enough to tide me over."

Tya chuckled. "It must be something special for you to be this excited about something other than loving me."

"Oh, it is." He glanced at her and grinned.

"Tell me?"

"Nope."

The traffic was light and it was barely twenty minutes when Blake turned into a large tract of land that was obviously under development for a housing estate.

"What is this?"

"This Tya is the current problematic low-cost housing project being run by my father's company."

"Why problematic?"

"It's complicated with costs and product, block sizes and required amenities."

"Won't it become a bit of a ghetto?"

Blake looked at her as he brought the car to a stop in front of a small office building. "Yes that's what the sociology experts are saying, Tya. It's a real danger. Most of the blocks are small with little or no backyards."

"That's not good for the future generations."

"No, Tya, but this is what is required to help ease the housing crisis. Come on hop out and I'll show you around."

Tya wasn't sure she wanted to look around. Lots of torn up ground and grass, stakes making blocks and roads. Even without a house the blocks looked small. She bit down on the words she wanted to say. She knew Blake had little choice in what he was managing.

He opened the door for her and she stepped up into the small neat air conditioned office. A tall darked haired man sat behind the desks tapping into the computer. In the corner was a model and on the walls were maps showing the blocks of land in the project.

"William this is my fiancé, Tya."

William stood and held out his hand. Tya took it. The grip was firm but brief. "Hi Tya nice to meet you."

Blake took her arm and steered her toward the model. This is the project. Peterson Flat.

Tya studied the model. She immediately noticed a couple of gaps where the tiny houses had been removed and discarded to the top of a nearby cupboard.

Blake pointed. "See these gaps? I've created them."

"Yes you have and not without some angst from everyone including your father."

Blake shrugged. "I know its reducing profits but I believe it's the right thing to do."

William frowned. "That remains to be seen."

Tya glanced from one man to the other. "Would you like to tell me what's going on and what it has to do with me."

Blake gently pushed her closer to the model with his hand in the center of her back. He pointed at the gaps. "I've created these gaps Tya especially for you."

She looked from the model to his. "What do I have to do with it."

Blake grinned. "As you said we are building low cost housing with the risk of forming ghettos."

"Yes."

"Well I have been so impressed with your idea of taking over vacant land to make gardens I thought I would include community gardens in the project. Three of them on the estate, already set up with beds and soil and facilities. On the edge of the playgrounds. So what do you think?"

Tya stared at the gaps in the model. Her head thudded and sparked a zing of excitement through her body. The love for this man burst through her. She had no idea he had taken her so seriously. He loved her but to go to this extent just blew her mind.

"Oh Blake this is amazing." She turned and hugged him. He held her against him for a long moment.

"He's trodden on lots of toes with this."

Tya stepped back from Blake and looked from one to the other. She sensed a level of tension in the room.

She looked up at Blake. "Is this a problem?"

Blake grinned. "It's not been without its problems, but we've worked through them haven't we William?"

Willaim grimaced. "We have. Blake has been determined."

"So you want to see them then you can plan the layouts and the facilities."

"Me?"

Blake smiled. "Who else would I get but my very own guerilla gardener."

"This will be so good. It will be legal, productive and foster a sense of community. Friendships and neighbors that know each other, fostering a sense of ownership and pride. I'd like to think it would reduce vandalism and even crime.

William patted Blake on the shoulder. "Yeah that's what the Boss said. I'm not so sure but I do believe it will be a positive for the residents. Plenty of social do gooders are already condemning these projects as leading to ghettoes of low-income disenchanted people. Anything that will redeem the perspective has got to be a good thing even if it comes at a cost."

"The cost is not so excessive. The project is still more than viable."

Tya felt vaguely uncomfortable standing between the two men. There was more going on than the words exchanged.

"Come on, Tya, let's take a look at your gardens" He handed her a hard hat and a pair of work boots. Tya pulled them on and they climbed into the car.

A short distance and Blake halted the car and climbed out. Tya followed him.

"Blake, I don't know what to say. I'm so excited that you have done this but William wasn't happy. Is that causing problems."

Blake grinned took her hand and led her into a large area of land. It was pegged out but not in blocks. "This is the playground and over here will be the garden. It's about two housing blocks and will have a fence and set beds like you have at Thistle Street and some raised beds, a watering system and sensor lights. So, what do you think?"

"It's incredible Blake thank you." Together they walked the area. As they returned Tya leapt into his arms. "Thank you, thank you. This is absolutely amazing."

They inspected each site. It was perfect. As they walked back to the car Tya hung onto Blake's arm. "We can do big beds and little. People could have their own beds and some for everyone. Can we put a barb-b-que in on the edge of the garden and playground for people to gather together." She rattled on about ideas and inclusions. Blake smiled as he helped her into the car.

"I'll give you the plans and you can design what you want but do remember there are limited funds."

She smiled. I'm used to doing things on a budget."

He kissed her.

"I'm working on the other developments. I'd like to see this sort of set up being incorporated in all our projects."

Tya sat tall. She was so excited and so proud of the man beside her. "You are amazing Blake."

***

They travelled back to the garden and picked up Endeva and Caitlin. Blake carried Caitlin inside after they wished Endeva good night. He stayed the night then headed home Sunday evening ready for work on Monday

"I'm going to miss you. Both of you. Are you sure this is what you want Tya? You could stay at my parents' place."

She nodded. With you back at work the house seems intimidating almost and your father needs peace and quiet to recover. A new baby in the house kinda disrupts that."

Blake grinned. "Very true our Caitlin does have a set of lungs on her especially when she's hungry. But I'll come here after I've help Alice with Dad each night. I've got used to having you be my side through the night and I don't want to sleep alone."

Tya stretched up and kissed his mouth. "So have I, but you won't get much sleep with Caitlin waking every few hours."

"Well if I'm here we can share the burden of the feeds and nappy changes."

"Are you sure?"

He nodded. Touched her mouth with his for one farewell kiss. "I'll see you tonight then, at the garden?"

Tya nodded. "Have a productive day, Blake."

***

When she could and the weather was suitable she would bundle Caitlin up in her baby carrier and work in the gardens beside Endeva.

Endeva was besotted begging to feed and change Caitlin and spoiling her with gifts of clothes and toys. "So, you're happy then?"

Tya smiled. "Oh, Endeva I'm so happy. Blake is a good man and his family...except one, have taken me to their hearts. I just wish Muir would get better. Caitlin is going to need a grandpa."

"I would never have believed it if I hadn't seen it with my own eyes. One like him marrying one like you. Truly though, I think he got the better deal."

"Oh, Endeva you're biased."

"Not at all my girl, not at all."

"Now we just have to wait for the family court to make its final decision on Caitlin. I don't think my brothers will try anything."

"Nah they wouldn't be that stupid."

Blake reassured her often that they would have no problems with custody but the tiny flicker of doubt would not be completely banished.

***

Muir had been home for nearly a month and making steady progress under Alice's tender care and was now heading back to the specialists for a follow up. If all went well at his father's appointment and once Blake had settled him and Alice back at home, he was going to pick her up for a meeting with Lyall to sort her mother's estate and for lunch.

The day dawned gloomy and humid. The Bureau of Metrology had predicted a one in a hundred-year rain event and widespread flash flooding. Tya peered out the front. It might be best to cancel lunch it wasn't good weather to be taking a baby out.

Blake, and Alice had already headed into town for Muir's appointment and Rhiana had caught the bus to university by the time the rain began. Blake or Alice might have to pick her up after her late afternoon lecture and tutorial

Tya's stomach churned while stinging pinpricks of fear raced over her skin as the rain fell in huge drops. There was no wind and the humidity clung to every pore making it almost unbearable.

The sweat glistened on Tya's skin as she settled Caitlin with a bottle after her bath. While Caitlin snoozed Tya hurried into her room, picked out her dress and slipped into the shower. She didn't feel that much fresher after a couple of minutes back in the thick humidity.

She slipped on her dress and grabbed her black court shoes from the wardrobe. Glancing outside she tugged off her dress and pulled on some stretchy navy pants and a thin cotton blouse with blue and white stripes. From the back of the wardrobe she hauled out a pair of light blue suede ankle boots. She had no intention of getting wet feet.

Tya heard a clatter. Startled and surprised by the sound she froze. A whisper of some undefined noise then the house was silent. She leapt up from the bed and raced from the bedroom. The sound of rain echoed loudly in the hall. Tya swung around. The front door was open and water was pouring onto the verandah and splashing into the hall.

She raced into the lounge.

"No no no." The capsule had gone.

The back door slammed. She raced toward it snatching it open to see Kyle stumbling down the garden path.

"Kyle! What the hell are you doing. Bring Caitlin back here now." Nausea washed over her.

Her brother clutched the capsule tighter as he glanced over his shoulder. He leered at her. "Give me back what is mine and you can have the brat."

"What Kyle? I don't have anything of yours. If I did you could have it. Give me back the baby." She lurched forward almost reaching him as he reached the gate.

She snatched out her phone.

Kyle halted. "No police or she dies. Do you hear me. No police."

"Kyle what the hell do you want? You can have it."

"I'll swap the brat for the house. It's not yours to have."

"What house?"

"My house. Our house. Mum's given it to you. You made her. You stole it from me. It was always supposed to be mine. She promised."

"Our house?"

"Don't act dumb sis you know what house."

Tya searched her mind but could not reconcile her brother's demands with reality.

"I'll swap her for the house." Kyle started to turn away.

Tya leapt at him her fingers clutching his shirt sleeve.

He jerked his arm away.

Tya hung on clawing at the ragged material.

He pulled away dragging her from her feet.

Her knees hit the wet pavement with a thud. She still clutched his sleeve even as she sprawled on the wet concrete.

He hauled her forward on her knees.

Her pants ripped on the rough surface. The sting as the stones gouged her skin from her kneecaps stabbed through her. She bit her lip against the cry of pain.

"Kyle stop. I'll give you anything, just give me Caitlin."

"Bitch. Conniving thieving bitch. You ain't getting her till I get the house."

He jerked his arm

The ragged material slipped through her fingers tearing into chunks as she tried to keep her grip.

He barged out the gate and began to run down the sidewalk. Tya scrambled to her feet and stumbled after him. "Kyle come back. There's no need for this."

"The house, Tya, the house," he shouted even as he continued to run.

Tears poured down her face. Tya swiped them away. She turned and stumbled back inside.

Silence encompassed her. She slumped into a kitchen chair, snatched her phone from the table and dialed Blake. No answer. She dialed Rhiana, no answer. She dialed 911 it rang out.

Her gut heaved and fury blasted through her. Kyle had taken Caitlin. What the hell was he talking about. What house? An ache of fear flooded through her. *Would he hurt her? Would he truly hurt a baby?* Tya knew if he was high on ice he might. *But what house?*

Suddenly recognition seeped into her mind. *Surely he didn't mean The Manor House. Her grandparents' house. That derelict old place. The place of long distant unhappy memories. But surely her mother didn't own it. She might have once, but surely it would have all gone on drugs.* Confusion speared through her. *Surely Kyle didn't think the old family home was still theirs. And if it was then her mother's will left it to her. Well, he could have it.*

She grabbed her phone and sent the same message to Blake and Rhiana. She tried 911 again it rang out.

Kyle has kidnapped Caitlin and taken her to our old house at Blacksmith's Gully. I'm going to get her back.

She snatched up the spare nappy bag stuffed it full of nappies and bottles filled with hot water and measured out the formula into the holder. She grabbed her raincoat and an umbrella, threw the stuff on the back seat of her car next to the capsule holder and backed out.

The rain pelted down on the windscreen. The wipers made little impact on the water even at full speed.

She turned her lights on even though it was only late morning. Despite her gut urging her to hurry Tya kept to a cautious speed as she could barely see the lines on the road. The roads were flooded. Storm water spilled from the gutters covering most of the road in some places. The traffic lights were out. She paused then dodged through the uncontrolled traffic her breath tight in her lungs. She skirted the city and found herself driving through a river of water at least a foot deep.

Her heart pounded. She gripped the wheel tightly terrified she was going to run off the road or into a piece of floating debris or another car. There were plenty of stalled vehicles with drivers leaning out of windows yelling for help.

As she turned up Gorge Road her foot hovered over the brake. Fear sat heavy in her chest. She hated this road at the best of times petrified of driving up the narrow winding road with the cliff rising one side and the gully falling away on the other side.

Tya peered through the windscreen for oncoming traffic and to make out the curves of the road. When headlights loomed she veered the car as close to the cliff as possible and the other car inched past. She moved on. There was no wind. The only sound was the car, the rain and her panicked breathing.

Trees loomed up on either side of the road their branches drooping under the weight of water on their leaves. She took a deep breath and prayed that the trees over hanging the side of the road would hold onto their branches. On each curve she could see the rain swollen creek in the bottom of the gully gushing and splashing between its banks. The flood water was rising.

She moved at a bit more than a crawl around curve after curve. A sense of isolation and loneliness embraced her for with clouds blocking the light and no sign of traffic in front or behind she might as well be the only one left on the earth. But she wasn't alone with Caitlin up ahead and the man she loved back in the city. She believed would come for her as soon as he could. She had a purpose and a port in a storm for which she was very grateful.

Every nerve in her body sizzled as she struggled to see ahead and keep her little car on the road.

At last she saw the sign. Blacksmith's Gully. She fought back tears of relief until the sobs and anger became a volatile mix in her chest. *Damn you to hell, Kyle, and you, Mum. You should have thought of this when you signed that bloody document. I don't want your inheritance I only ever wanted what you could not give me, a mother's love. A chance to give that to Caitlin.*

Tears slipped down over her chilled cheeks. She swiped them away. Pinpricks of light glowed through the rain. The lights of the few houses in town. She wound her way through town, turned right and pushed her little car to climb the hill. Barely a kilometer up the hill, she turned onto a dirt road and headed back down into a gully. The red dirt track was a slippery strip of chewed up mud. The tracks of another vehicle stood out like a beacon. Kyle's tracks. The middle hump scratched along the bottom of her car.

The car slewed to the right. Tya instinctively over corrected, then again until she finally got back on the straight and narrow. The car crawled forward. Suddenly the wheels spun. The engine roared. She lifted her foot off the accelerator then applied it again terrified of getting bogged. The car rushed forward.

The shadowy bulk of the house loomed dark and menacing off to the right. Cautiously she turned toward it. No light glowed. Uncertainty and fear wrapped stinging tentacles around her. *Had Kyle tricked her? But where was Caitlin?* She shivered as she pulled up by the side of the house. Immediately she picked up her phone. No signal and no messages. Her heart felt heavy in her chest even though she knew Blake would come if he could. The state of the road had been treacherous. Maybe she was all on her own. The doubt niggled but she pushed it away. Blake would come to her aid. She took a deep breath and continued to the house.

Rain continued to pelt down. The disrepair of the house stood out starkly as she neared it. Ready to be condemned she guessed. The eaves and gutters hung down. Water poured in torrents from the roof. The verandah posts looked rotten. Glass panels in the windows were broken. This was no place for a baby.

The rain eased for a moment and Tya glimpsed a red four-wheel drive's bonnet jutting out from behind the house. She didn't recognize the car, but it had to be Kyle. Trepidation shivered through her as she pulled on her raincoat and climbed out of the car. She swung the nappy bag over her shoulder. Hunched against the deluge she walked toward the house. The door swung drunkenly on its hinges as she pushed it open. The old house creaked. Loose wooden slats on the walls creaked under the weight of water. 'Kyle I'm here. Alone, but others are coming."

Silence except for the rain.

"Kyle, give me Caitlin. And I'll go away. You can have the house I don't want it. I never wanted it."

She walked cautiously around the rooms. Old furniture littered the room. Rain trickled in the broken windows and through the roof.

She went back to the front door. "Kyle," she screamed.

A door slammed. Tya leaped off the verandah. Kyle loomed up in front of her.

"Where's Caitlin?"

"She's safe, Sis. Safe from you and your grasping boyfriend. You can have her, but the house is mine. Do you understand? It's mine, not yours."

"Kyle you can have the house but please let me see her. I need to know Caitlin is okay.'

He stepped closer, leering, his hands deep in his jean's pockets. "Ain't gonna hurt her. You sign the papers for the house and you can have her.'

"Kyle it will takes a few days to sign the house over. I didn't rush because Mum had nothing to leave. I haven't even talked to the lawyer yet. Caitlin cannot stay here until then. Please Kyle give her to me."

He laughed at her pleading. Suddenly the rain stopped. Silence enveloped them.

Tya heard the tiniest mewling sound. She turned and ran. Kyle was right behind her. His gasping breaths rasped in the still wet air. Tya scrambled over the stone wall that once edged the garden. Three steps and she threw herself on the old cellar doors. She scrabbled at the rusty latch with wet hands. The mewling sounded louder, more frantic.

The bastard had her in the cellar. It was no place for a baby. For anyone. Moldy, damp, prone to flooding and populated with spiders, scorpions, and centipedes.

Tya wrenched the door open. It creaked against her efforts.

Kyle stood back laughing at her desperate efforts but made no attempt to stop her.

Warning bells rang in her mind. She turned to look at him. It wouldn't be the first time he had locked someone in the cellar.

The cries of the baby sliced through the deadly tension between them. Tya hauled the door open and peered into the darkness. She could hear Caitlin, close now. She climbed into the cellar and using her phone torch she searched shocked to find she was wading through water above her ankles.

"Kyle, you bastard. How could you? Help me get her out. Its flooding in here."

Silence met her anguished plea. She heard the cry and spun around. Caitlin was still in the capsule the blanket around her flicking and jumping in the tiny beam of light as the child screamed in frustration and hunger. Tya scooped the capsule up and ran towards the door. She climbed the rough wooden steps but just as her head came level with the door frame the door slammed shut cracking her on the top of the head.

She staggered, tightened her grip on the capsule with one hand and clutched at the wooden steps with the other. Darkness swirled around her. Her foot slipped and she slid into the water. Now knee deep.

"Kyle. Don't so this. Kyle help me."

Nothing

She climbed the two bottom steps and put the capsule on the third step. Caitlin screamed.

Tya shushed her and search for a dummy. There was none in the capsule. She clung to the wooden step with one hand and swinging the nappy bag around undid the zip and scrabbled around with her hand until her fingers finally closed over a dummy. She pulled it out and put it into Caitlin's mouth. The baby sucked hard but continued to cry softly.

"Kyle. Let me out."

She reached up and bashed on the cellar door but when she brought down a shower of moldering wet wood on top of them she stopped and reassessed the situation.

Water trickled and gurgled behind her. The water came through the door in cold rivulets drenching her from head to toe.

Something ran over her hand. She screamed and shook her hand. Whatever it was went flying.

I have to get out of here. I have to get Caitlin out. I am not going to die when I have just found love.

She moved the capsule to one side and proceeded to bang on the other side of the cellar door. Wet rotting wood showered down on her. She banged again. Her fists throbbed but now she could see grey light through the cracks in the wood.

Caitlin proceeded to scream.

"Oh, little darling, don't cry. Tya will get us out. Blake will come and get us. Shhh. Shhh."

But Caitlin would not be soothed. Adjusting her footing Tya swung the nappy bag onto the step by the capsule. With one hand she managed to fish out a bottle of water. It was just warm. She tucked it into the pocket of her raincoat and dug down for the measured dose of formula. She struggled to get both the bottle and the formula container open but eventually she managed to tip the formula into the bottle. Some spilled but Tya figured even if it was a fraction thin it would soothe Caitlin. She shook the bottle and hoped all the formula was dissolved as she pulled the dummy out and gave the baby the bottle. The screaming stopped and Caitlin suckled strongly. Tears flooded Tya's eyes. *Dear little bubba.*

It took quite a while before Caitlin was satisfied and Tya waited with barely held in check impatience.

The water was still running into the cellar. Anxious about testing the water level Tya reluctantly dipped her foot down and gasped. The water lapped barely a foot below the step she stood on.

Oh God its rising fast.

"Kyle for God's sake open the door. We're going to drown."

Silence except the ominous sound of running water and pounding rain.

She dug out her phone but shoved it back into her pocket frustrated, angry and afraid at the lack of bars.

She gazed at Caitlin's sweet little face pale in the grey light. There is no way I'm losing her or drowning. *Damn you, Kyle.* She cast around in the grey light. She needed a tool, to batter the door open.

Tya secured the capsule on the step and carefully lowered herself into the water. It was icy cold in comparison to the humid moldy air of the cellar. She looked around using her phone torch. It didn't make much of an impression on the darkness. She waded slowly trying to remember what they had kept in the cellar. After it flooded the first time when she was a small child not much. A grey pitted handle leaned against the wall. Tya grabbed it and lifted. It was a metal garden rake. The handle was pretty rotten but the metal rake end was still intact. She raised it above the water and waded back to the steps. Icy shivers ran through her and she flexed her fingers to ensure they were still moving. Back on the step she slammed the rake handle against the door. Damp wood rained down. Caitlin flinched at the noise but didn't wake. Tya slammed it again. More wood rained down. And again. The handle snapped. Splinters stabbed into her palm.

"Ouch. Ouch. Damn."

She smashed the remaining rake handle against the step. It broke away. Tya stretched up and rammed the rake head into the timbers. It broke through. She dragged on it and tore a whole chuck of wood free.

"Yay. We doing it Caitlin."

The water was now lapping around her knees. They didn't have much time. She strangled the sobs pushing up in her chest and slammed the rake head at the door again. More timber broke free.

Caitlin woke and whimpered.

Tya shoved the dummy in her mouth.

She continued to whimper.

There was no time to soothe her. With a significant gap Tya pushed the rake head through and using the prongs as hooks dragged the wood down. A huge chunk broke off. Tya wavered on the step, swaying back and forth. She snatched at the next step. Her fingers slipped. She scrabbled her feet but already her body was dropping. She flailed with her arms and legs but moments later the cold dirty water closed over her head.

Tya flapped her arms panic rising in a chilled wall of darkness. Instinctively she kept a tight grip on the rake head. She couldn't touch the bottom, and her raincoat hampered her swimming technique. Desperation crunched in her gut as panic squeezed her lungs. Crunching her teeth together and holding what little breath she had Tya kicked her legs at a furious beat until she finally bobbed to the surface. She gasped for air and clumsily paddled back to the steps.

Cold water had splashed over Caitlin and she was screaming, her little face screwed up and red.

Her first instinct was to comfort her but she pushed it down and scrambled up the submerged steps to attack the wood.

Large chunks came away. The water had risen significantly. She grabbed the capsule but couldn't get it through the hole. She unclipped Caitlin and cuddling the screaming baby to her breasts she scrambled up on the slippery steps using the rusting hinge of the door where the wood had fallen away. Holding her breath she hauled the top half of herself and Caitlin through the jagged gap. She lost her footing but hung onto the edge of the door and the hinge.

I'll never get out. Oh God, I can't heave myself up. The water swirled around her in an icy wave. She was scared to call out. She glanced around. There was no sign of Kyle but she could see the bonnet of his car still pocking out from behind the corner of the house.

A grumble of a powerful motor rose above the rain. She peered through the rain. If Kyle was to come now he might push her back in.

Lights pierced the gloom and swung in an arch. A white four by four loomed through the pelting rain.

Relief washed over her. Oh my God, Blake. Blake's here. Do you hear that Caitlin sweetheart. Blake's here.

The car slammed to a halt and driver's door flung open.

'Tya. Tya. Answer me. Are you here?"

"I'm here Blake. At the cellar door."

"Tya, my love.' Blake swung in her direction. Running and leaping over the grass and through the mud.

Tears burn hot steams down her cheeks. "Blake. Oh thank God you've come."

His hand scooped under her arms and he was hauling them up through the door. Caitlin screamed between them as he held her tight.

"Oh my God I thought I'd lost you."

"I was afraid the floods would stop you coming."

"I'll never stop coming to save you Tya. I've called the police, but the whole city is a disaster. Blackouts, floods and accidents. So I don't know when they are coming, if they are coming."

"We have to get Caitlin to hospital. She's been the cold cellar for hours and she's all wet."

"Come, Tya, lets go."

"We need the capsule."

Blake leaned into the gap and tugged the capsule turning it sideways to drag it through the gap.

They climbed into Blake's car with Caitlin settled in the capsule with Tya beside her in the back seat.

He turned the heating on and in the seats.

"I have the nappy bag can you change her while I drive."

"Drive carefully."

Blake revved the engine and took off. The car slid in the mud and Blake adjusted the driving options. They moved forward. A glare of lights on high beam highlighted the car. The roar of an engine filled the air.

"Blake go. Go! Its Kyle. He's going to ram us."

As Blake accelerated the red car slammed into Blake's door. Tya threw herself across the baby feeling shards of glass splatter on her back. The scream of tortured metal and the clatter of shattered glass filled the air as the red car pushed their car off the track and into a muddy ditch. Steam rose from the engine of the red car. The engine screeched in acceleration but neither car moved.

"Blake are you alright?"

He groaned.

"Answer me Blake?"

"I'm okay Tya. Are you and Caitlin okay?"

"Yes, we're both fine."

"I don't think my car is drivable Tya."

"Then we'll use mine it's around the front." Tya was already getting out of the car as she spoke.

"I don't think I can make it Tya. My leg is hurting bad. Take Caitlin and go."

"No. I'm not leaving you with that drug addled mad man."

She walked around the red car and saw her brother slumped in the seat. He was conscious. He looked up at her.

"I'll stop you, Tya. I'll get the house. It's mine."

The madness of the drugs made his eyes glitter. Droplets of water ran down his pale skin. Tya didn't know if it was sweat or rain and didn't care. Terror clutched her chest at what he might do next. They needed to get away.

"Bastard. Stupid bastard." She screamed and ran in the direction of her car. She revved it and reversed up by the passenger side of Blake's car.

She squeezed out between the cars. Caitlin was screaming. Blake hadn't moved.

Tya dragged the door open. "Blake tell me you're okay."

"I'm a bit broken Tya best leave me, I'll manage."

"No."

Kyle revved the engine of the car trying to reverse and untangle his vehicle from the collision.

"We have to go Blake. I think he's going to have another go.

Blake nodded. "Help me get out and we'll go."

Tya climbed in the front seat undid the seat belt and Blake managed to ease himself out from the steering wheel and side airbag.

"Owww." He clutched his side with his right arm. "I think my ribs are broken and I know my arm and leg are."

Tya grabbed the capsule and slapped it in place in her car.

She reached in and hauled Blake out the door. He balanced on one leg as she almost threw him into the back seat.

He yelped in pain.

The red car began to move backwards dragging Blake's car with it.

Tya screamed almost caught by the open door as she tumbled into the driver's seat and pressed the accelerator slowly easing the idling car forward.

An inhuman screech rent the air. Tya glanced over her shoulder to see the red car loosen from Blake's and shoot backwards. Almost immediately it jumped forward again ramming Blake's car again right in the driver's door.

Tya stepped on the accelerator her car just slipping out of the way of Blake's car as Kyle shoved it forward right across the driveway and over a low stone fence. She let out a squeak of terror and relief as they hurtled down the driveway. When she entered town, she stopped. No lights loomed behind her. She suspected, hoped, that Kyle's car would not be drivable. She parked in under a willow tree and turned the lights off but left the engine idling in case she needed to make a quick getaway. She climbed out of the driver's side and went around to Cailtin. With hurried movements she stripped the baby and with her screaming hysterically Tya dressed her in dry clothes and re-strapped her in the capsule. She dug out a bottle of tepid water and with shaky hands added the formula.

She placed the bottle in Caitlin's mouth. "Can you manage to feed Caitlin?"

"I can," Blake muttered through a groan and reached over to hold the bottle.

"Is it bad Blake?"

"It hurts like hell but don't worry about me just drive and be careful." She slipped into the driver's seat scanned the surrounds and eased out from the concealing tree.

The rain had eased to splattering drops and the windscreen wipers kept the glass relatively clear. At one intersection she glanced in the back at her two silent passengers. Cailtin was lying with her eyes open and sucking contentedly on Blake's little finger. Blake was gazing down at her. Tya could see the love reflected in his expression despite the winces of pain.

She dialed the emergency number and jerkily updated the police. Then spoke to the ambulance service and explained about Blake. She could barely talk her teeth chattering with the terrible cold seeping into her bones.

The ambulance phone attendee was less than positive. "I'm sorry love, all our ambulances are ramped at the RAH or on the road. It's chaos all round the city. I'm not sure if they can get through, everywhere has flash flooding. I'm not sure how long they will be. Is it life threatening."

"Yes. My fiancé has been in an accident I think he has broken arm, leg and maybe ribs or internal injuries."

"Where are you exactly?"

"I'm just coming down Gorge Road."

"We'll get an ambulance there as soon as we can, but its bedlam with so many needing help. Keep him warm. Do first aid."

Tya drove with care as fast as she could.

It seemed to take forever to reach the hospital but at last they veered into the ER parking lot. Moments later two nurses and a porter brought a gurney out and transferred Blake.

Blake sagged back on the gurney and closed his eyes. They pushed the gurney through the doors across the ER and straight into a treatment room. Tya arranged for Caitlin to be looked at then called Rhiana. Relief flooded through her when she answered.

"I'm with Mum now she picked me up from Uni because they closed and sent us home. We'll be there in short while."

Half an hour later Alice and Rhiana joined her in the waiting room. Tya paced. Blake was still in surgery when they arrived. Caitlin was sleeping with a drip in her tiny arm. Dehydration was her main problem and mild hypothermia.

The time passed slowly until finally the doctor arrived.

"Thankfully his injuries, while extensive and could have been life threatening are all repairable. He's out of surgery and you can go and see him just for a few minutes."

They all went in, approaching the bed tentatively.

The machines clicked and sighed. Blake had his right leg in a cast with metal frames sticking out of his skin. His head was bandaged and his shoulder dangled in a special hanging sling.

His face was bruised and swollen. He opened his eyes and tried to smile through the gashed lip.

"Blake, my love, how are you feeling?"

"Pretty rotten actually. It hurts everywhere. How's Caitlin?"

Tya smiled. "She's a bit dehydrated and a bit cold but otherwise none the worse for her experience.

Alice was already on the phone to Muir. She put him on the loud speaker.

"You given us a pretty bad scare, son. Are you all right Tya and what about Caitlin?"

"Yes. We are both fine."

Shortly after the police arrived and Tya went with them to answer all their questions. Blake's input could wait until he felt better.

The police informed Tya her brother had passed from either an overdose or his injuries.

Tya felt a small wave of sadness waft over her. Poor Kyle never had a chance.

When she returned to Blake's room Talisha sat outside. Tya glowered at her.

Talisha looked down at her feet.

Tya noticed the tears on her cheeks before she did.

Talisha looked up at Tya. "Mum won't let me go in. She says I don't deserve it. I'm so sorry Tya. To make such a mistake. To treat my brother to abysmally. I hope you can both forgive me, one day.

Tya shook her head. "I don't know Talisha whether Blake will forgive you but for now he does not need you in his life. Perhaps one day. It would be best if you left."

Tears streamed down her cheeks, her make up smeared and her nose ran. She sniffed inelegantly as she rose to her feet. "Tell him I'm sorry."

Tya stood there and watched her walk away before she returned to Blake's bedside.

***

Dave helped Tya out of the car.

Rhiana fluffed Tya's dress and carefully spread out her train.

The music began to play. It was her cue.

She tucked her hand in Dave's elbow and together they walked into the church.

The pews were lined with roses and bows in apricot and lemon. They moved slowly down the aisle. At the alter Blake stood resplendent in his dark suit. Off to the side Tya could see Alice holding Caitlin, now almost six months old. She was dressed in the prettiest lemon dress with a garland of flowers around her head. On the other side sat Endeva, the boys from Thistle Street and the all the other guerrilla gardeners. The rest of the pews were filled with Blake's friends and associates. Tya's heart swelled with joy and for the first time in her life she felt worthy of all the good in her life.

ALSO BY

Adult Fantasy: writing as Emily Tyler
Thrones of Annaticcia series
Book 1: TWIN BETRAYAL

Princess Rosin, legitimate only daughter of the royal marriage is destined to be Queen of Keswin but her twin, Ciara covets the crown. Her lover, Lord Devon also wants the crown and he seizes it in a bloody coup.

While fleeing to safety, Rosin saves and falls in love with a wounded soldier, Arlan, and when no noble will offer marriage, she becomes determined to marry the man she loves.

But Rosin knows she must soon put their potential happiness aside and return to save her throne.

Book 2: RETRIBUTION & RESTITUTION

With Arlan by her side can Rosin save her realm, defeat Devon and defy the High Queen?

Rosin rails against waiting for the tidal wash determined to save Keswin. On the cusp of the freeze, she enlists the help of Trystan, maligned Dominus of Sanjeva and Lukaz, a Gaudi male, to build a Gaudi ponkini and cross the river. The river almost drowns her, and an avalanche buries her consort and commanders.

Rosin, Arlan and her warriors travel via a secret canyon through the mountains to Cottam Village where with the help of the High Queen's Battalion they defeat Devon's army. Garrett tries to kidnap her for Devon. Rosin's strength and determination in the face of adversity captures the respect and loyalty of her Commanders Carrick and Trystan, her warriors and the people of Cottam. Commander Ryne, Isolde's grandson, confirms Arlan is his former common blood warrior, Quinnlan and an unsuitable consort for Rosin. Ryne oversteps his position and charges Arlan with dereliction of duty and treason. Rosin asserts her authority to bring the needed cooperation for their survival.

The few who remain at the castle have mixed feelings about her return and Rosin faces the monstrous truth about her parents' rule. A bitter insider helps Devon kidnap her again. She escapes but miscarries her child. Rosin vows she will not live under Devon's threat and together with Arlan she plans revenge for his abominations and the murder of her child.

Dykarin Dragon Shifters
Book 1: ANARCHY

Taminsha, Regent of Aikanshin is broken and dying from Nyket's savage attack, but she must survive to fulfil her destiny and save Dykarin from the Era of Darkness.

Death and grief stalk her. Love and peace are transient gifts in the midst of Nyket's tryanny.

Already stripped of all that matters Taminisha's will to live is crushed when Nyket cruelly uses her body to breed an heir.

Nyket snatches the newborn from her breast and tries to kill Taminisha. But she escapes with the help of Khoury and the mysterious child Kashwen.

Gravley injured she crash lands on Oventi Island, and stalked from above by Nyket, she begs Spirit to take her hand end her misery.

Book 2 SANCTUARY

The fight is no longer about equality but subjugation.

When Taminisha crash lands on Oventi she finds sanctuary instead of death with Khimaera outcasts and the three Siblings.

But that security is threatened as Nyket continues to ravage Dykarin but resistance against him is building.

Rabikan falls to Nyket as Adakan rescues his soulmate Jycosa and flees back to the sanctuary of Mitikan, the only clan still free of the scourge of Nyket.

In Mitikan with Guardian Okeyon's assistance Larkin rallies the Khimaera, refugees and surviving Ellkiiyn to train and prepare for a final battle against Nyket.

Tarlitek brings Jabrikan, the young heir apparent of Aikanshin, out of hiding to lead all Ellkiiyn to freedom and restore the true Guardians of the Clans and kill Nyket.

Erotic Romance: writing as Cassandra Hawke
BLOOD TIES A BROKEN HEART
(stand alone)

When Rylee returns to Adelaide to take over her God-mother's stables, seeing Ashford St Clair brings back memories of past events—when he'd sacrificed his promising equestrian career and alienated Rylee in the process. Ash is determined to win Rylee back and they reach an uneasy compromise when their passion for each other is re-ignited.

But the deeds of the past still haunt the present threatening their relationship. An old enemy returns to cause trouble for Rylee—Ash's sister, Arden—the one who brought about Ash's downfall in the first place. She makes it clear that there is no room for Rylee in Ash's life and she'll do anything to make sure the lovers remain apart.

Will Rylee come to terms with the mistakes she and Ash made in the past and learn to love and trust each other again?

DEMOLITION OF THE HEART
(stand alone)

Kayla Mackenzie is shocked when she finds out the man she has just made passionate love to the man is responsible for her priceless paintings being in a charity auction and intends to demolish her beloved family home.

Wade has no idea that his inheritance of historical Ainsley House has been carefully orchestrated and that he is a pawn in a complex plot that will not only deprive Kayla of her beloved family home and her inheritance, but also her life. The thing he hadn't counted on was the impetus of fiery-tempered Kayla stealing his well-guarded heart before he even knew it was at risk.

Their confrontations are fierce and explosive and they both determinedly maintain joint residence of the historic house, but they find themselves fighting an entirely different battle as the smoldering attraction between them erupts into an inferno of desire and sexual attraction. They finally get to the truth of how the house came to be in Wade's hands and Kayla claims her inheritance and strikes a business deal with Wade that will save the house.

DEATHLY EMBRACE
(stand alone)

The ghost of Annie Dunsford is beautiful, passionate and deadly. Revenge is her goal. Sex is her weapon. Logan is her victim. Unless Paige and the unexpected passion he has found with her can save him.

A surprise joint inheritance requires Logan and Paige to live together in the old haunted house for a year. It all seems simple enough. But it is not simple at all.

The ghost of Annie Dunsford haunts the place. Out for revenge the beautiful and deadly Annie seduces Logan and their steamy passionate sexual encounters suck the life out of him leaving him sexually frustrated, drained and afraid to sleep alone.

Logan's vulnerability sparks something deep in Paige's soul and the sexual attraction simmering between them explodes into molten hot sex. The ghost is furious at the emotions developing between Logan and Paige, and they find themselves fighting for their lives. Their joint struggle to survive the ghost's fury and demands for justice brings

them closer together and sparks an unexpected passionate new love.
But is that love strong enough to save their lives from a spirit who wants only their deaths.

ACKNOWLEDGEMENTS

Mary Gudzenovs : Digital formatting
Mary Gudzenovs : Cover design

About the Author

About the Author- DionieMcNair
Writing as DionieMcNair (YA), Emily Tyler (Fantasy) & Cassandra Hawke (Romance)

Dionie was a closet writer for several years before she got brave enough to share her work with anyone. At 24, she joined Eyre Writers Inc, a creative writing group in the seaside town of Port Lincoln, Soth Australia. Her first book was a 100,000 word family saga.

Her book was not published and as she spent more time with the writers group she discovered why. Her writing was raw, wordy, and lacking in finesse. She desperately wanted to be a writer and set out to improve her writing by attending workshops and classes whenever they were offered. And improve she did.

After a workshop on 'How to write a Mills and Boon', she embarked on a new direction—writing the romance novel, but even with significant improvements in her style, publication remained elusive. After studying children's literature at university Dionie wrote the first draft of a

Young Adult novel, but despite several re-drafts, it remained unpublished.

For a while, life—raising three children, a marriage breakup, and studying—got in the way and writing was temporarily abandoned. Dionie went onto work in marketing and fundraising for five years and then moved to Volunteer Management with a large not-for-profit. But the stories remained in her head and eventually one cried to be released onto paper. So she took up the pen again (or the computer keyboard, as it was this time).

After being made redundant from the job she loved in 2011 Dionie became a carer for her frail, vision-impaired mother and turned to fulfilling her dream of becoming a writer. Two years later, her first book was accepted for publication. It was a heart stopping moment and the realisation of a life long dream.

When Dionie is not writing I enjoy spending time with my family and friends, especially my mother, and my three wonderful adult children and four adorable grandchildren.

Dionie also enjoys egg decorating and carving, reading, of course, painting, cooking and archery.